THE BLOOD SAMPLE

YEMI ADEBIYI

*AuthorHouse™ UK
1663 Liberty Drive
Bloomington, IN 47403 USA
www.authorhouse.co.uk
Phone: 0800.197.4150*

This story is a work of fiction. All characters and places mentioned were created by the author. Any coincidences with real persons and places were not intended.

Published by AuthorHouse 03/10/2014

*ISBN: 978-1-4918-9774-4 (sc)
ISBN: 978-1-4918-9775-1 (e)*

Print information available on the last page.

'That's the big question, Your Excellency.' Tony responded. 'Knowing who did it would not change the situation because the evidence is gone.' You have only one option.' He stopped.

'What's the option?'

'Go for the HIV test if you are sure it will be negative. If otherwise, all the crimes, allegedly committed by Idoh would be placed on your doorstep. Your personal assistant will be seen as an accomplice.'

Mark looked thoughtful. 'I think I will do that.'

Envoy Tony Whitesand stood up to go as Mark stopped pacing the room. He peeped through the window curtain and saw a bird trying to walk on the artificial lake. Suddenly, water from the fountain splashed on its body. In its attempt to take off, it slid further into the lake and started to drift with the induced water current. How will it get itself out of the wet situation? Mark was full of pity for the bird that could not use its wet wings and entangled legs. He tried to force a smile as he reflected on his own predicament . . . .

For
Joseph Fashoro
Benson Akingboye
Micheal Famuyide

It was election year in the oil-rich state of Zowambia and the incumbent President, Mark Okuta, wanted to run again. He was convinced he needed a second term to consolidate on the gains of his fiscal and economic reforms that were applauded by indigenous and foreign investors. Party politics was in full swing; some politicians playing the game with artistic masterstroke and some pursuing it with craftsman's mediocrity. In all, the beats were growing louder and the political heat becoming intense as Zowambia got closer to election month.

'Our party's primary is going to be very competitive.' President Okuta commented as his wife poured hot coffee into his cup.

'You will triumph, darling.' First Lady Maggy Okuta assured him.

'My opponents within the party are formidable.'

'The incumbent factor will work in your favour.' Maggy reassured him of victory.

Mark was thoughtful. He knew that if he scaled the hurdle of the presidential primaries of the Zowambia National Party, he had to further impress the electorate. He could not rely, solely, on the advantages of incumbency to fight the opposition candidate at the polls. Funny enough, he knew who would be the flag bearer of the Democratic Party. He would need a popular manifesto for his campaign to defeat Yusuf Naibawa at the polls.

One of his strategies to boost his image and that of the administration was to involve women in his administration. Thus, he appointed two women to ministerial positions and gave his wife more roles to play in government

Conferences on women interests were organized in the three major regions; Zom, Wam and Biam. In addition, the political hotbed cities, Golas and Longbridge, gave priority to female-friendly programmes.

It was during one of such women conferences that the vehicles in the convoy of the First Lady got involved in a multiple accident inside the city of Longbridge on their way to the seat of Government, Seaview City. First Lady Maggy Okuta and one of the delegates from Ashanti, a neighbouring West African country were seriously injured. They were rushed to the National Hospital's intensive care unit. Both of them needed blood transfusion to replace the heavy loss of blood from their system.

The blood group of Maggy Okuta was not known. Neither the President nor the President's physician could be reached. They were far away in Zurich at a meeting organized by World Health Organization. The National Hospital's director ordered a blood test, to ascertain her blood group. As it was the norm, allied tests had to go with it.

It was about ten hours before Maggy's condition became stable. The next day, she was flown out of Zowambia to Europe. Her Excellency's life is precious.

xxxxx

The President hurriedly abandoned the Zurich gathering to visit his wife at Embassy Hospital in London. When he was alone with the foreign doctor, he was eager to know how long it will take Maggy to recover fully.

'She is going to be alright, Mr. President' Dr Ivy Douglas said and paused. 'But she is likely to have her resistance against her original condition affected.'

'What original condition?' President Mark was lost.

'Her status.'

'I don't understand you, doctor.'

It was the doctor's turn in the game of puzzle as he looked at the President. 'You must know your wife is a carrier of human immune deficiency virus, HIV, Mr. President.'

'I am shocked at hearing this, doctor.' There was pain written all over the face of President Okuta. 'Did you carry out a test on her?'

'I didn't, Sir. It is there in coded form in her medical report from the National Hospital in Longbridge.' The doctor looked intensely at the President. Was he acting or pretending? She saw frantic worries and panic, tell-tale traits of a patient with a newly discovered ailment

'I am not sure my wife knows about her condition.' It was more of a soliloquy.

'You may be right, Mr. President. The result of the blood test on her after the accident confirmed her HIV status. It is absurd that you were not told.'

'I had a long chat with the doctor in charge. Her status was not mentioned. It's really absurd.'

Doctor Douglas looked at the President thoughtfully before speaking again. 'May be Dr Fred Agbamuche wanted your personal physician to inform you.'

'I don't think he told my doctor. If Fred did, I would have known immediately. Let me find out from him.' President Okuta dialed the number of his medical aide as Ivy left the room.

'Your Excellency.' Doctor Idoh Bibilari took his call.

The President drawled over what to ask his doctor as he suddenly realised the gravity of the budding scandal of the HIV-status of the First Lady. The grim prospect was enough to nail his political coffin. 'Did Fred tell you of any other health problem of Maggie?'

Idoh reviewed his discussion with the National Hospital Director before answering the question. 'Fred didn't tell me, Sir.'

'Okay.'

Idoh was puzzled. 'Is there anything wrong apart from the accident, Sir?'

'What else do you expect? Maggie and the whole family is your responsibility, Doctor.' The President quipped.

'She told me last week that she might be pregnant.'

'She hadn't told me.' President Okuta sounded offended.

'She wanted to be sure and would want to know the sex of the baby if she were truly pregnant before getting you involved.'

'You were planning abortion of my baby if it happened to be a girl, and without my knowledge.' There was rage in the President's voice. Dr. Bibilari noticed this.

'I wouldn't know Her Excellency's plan if she was truly pregnant.' Idoh paused. 'But I would have told you immediately I confirmed her pregnancy. Even against her wish.' Idoh's voice was convincing.

'Don't mind my outpouring IB,' the President told his medical aide in a manner to reassure him all was well between them. 'Maggy wants a boy. I have told her I am okay with Perpetual, Agatha and Lucia. They are three lovely, beautiful girls.' He cut off the conversation as Ivy re-entered the room.

He turned to Ivy. 'Is there anybody apart from you, who knows about this deadly condition of my wife?

'I opened the sealed file from Longbridge. The nurses' attention has been on post-accident treatments. Besides, a new folder was opened here with the history of treatments already administered in Zowambia. No one knows about the HIV yet.' She stopped and looked at the President enquiringly.

President Okuta smiled. He was inwardly grateful that only Ivy knew about the ailment. He had to find a way to talk her into silence over disclosing it to the public. For a minute or thereabout, he was silent, thinking.

Doctor Ivy Douglas noticed this and decided to allow him to be alone in the private room with his wife placed on heavy sedative. 'I need to give you time to think on what next, Sir.' Ivy walked to the door.

'Doctor Douglas.' The President called her as she was opening the door. 'Please, don't go yet. I have something important to discuss with you.'

'Your wish is my command, Sir.' She turned back from the door and smiled, hoping that her disposition would help to relax the visible tension on the President.

'I need your help and cooperation, doctor.' Mark said, and paused. When he was sure of her complete attention, he continued. 'I don't want anybody else to know about the HIV status of my wife.' He stopped and looked straight into her eyes. 'I want to buy some time before the scandal is made public.'

'Why, Mr. President?' Without waiting for an answer she spoke further, candidly. 'Your wish is against medical ethics. Do you know that there is a high probability of His Excellency being HIV positive?'

'I thought of it already, but that's not my reason. HIV positive status does not make one an automatic AIDS patient. At least, Maggy looked healthy, and I, too. But my reason is political. I am running for a second term. This news might blow my chance of winning the election. The social stigma attached to HIV positive person in Zowambia is enormous. There could be no political success for an HIV candidate or the husband of a HIV-positive wife. And I intend to contest and win the next election.' Mark stopped and studied her countenance. She was all professional, he thought. Not a single sign of emotion was discernable in her look.

'It is against medical ethics if I don't mention this in my report. In fact, your wife must commence treatment on the ailment, too.' She knew the President did not like what she said. She tried to make him see reason with her. 'Anyway, we could keep the information until she is completely stable in order to commence treatment. That's what your Doctor Fred would have done. He must have realised the need to play down on the First Lady's ailment hence, the way it was hidden in the report. The important and ethical thing to do is to spell it out. And Doctor Fred did. If I don't pass the information down to your physician, Dr. Fred's report will do so. The truth will be out before long, Sir.'

The President was relieved. 'Thank you Doctor. Give me some time to sort things out with IB. You can let me have the folder from Zowambia. I will summon Dr Fred to London. The three of you must do something to keep me out of this medical mess.'

Dr. Ivy Douglas was reluctant to hand over the medical report. 'We don't have a copy yet.'

'You don't have to, Doctor.' President Mark Okuta said with authority. 'I want to be sure you do not have evidence to show if you decided to make her status known to the public before I am ready for such.'

The lady doctor saw the threat in the President's voice. 'You can have it. But, in case it is discovered missing before you return it, I will not own up that I released it. In addition,

I will be emphatic that His Excellency is a suspect. At least you were looking at it when I was leaving the room during this first meeting.'

'That's okay with me.'

'As you please, Your Excellency.'

President Mark Okuta was looking at all the medical jargons in the folder from Zowambia when Doctor Ivy Douglas left the room and headed straight to see the next patient. She was relieved that she had to attend to an ordinary citizen next, not a VIP.

xxxxx

The President sat down and studied the relaxed face of her sleeping wife and shook his head. The news would devastate her, he thought. Was she having an affair with somebody else? Was it his own escapade, the secretly arranged meeting with supposedly HIV-free, white lady that entertained him after the UN assembly programme, that bought this calamity to his wife, his family? If she was pregnant, the unborn baby would be HIV positive. That would be as long as the secret could be kept. Thoughts raged on, in his mind.

The wife stirred in her sleep. He expectantly checked to know whether she was awake. She was not. He took the folder in his left hand covered with the *agbada* he wore and stepped out into the corridor where his presidential guards were waiting.

Back to the Presidential suite of the Zowambia Lodge in Central London, President Mark Okuta put a call to the Director of National Hospital at Longbridge. He was woken up by the burr and felt reluctant to take the call. When he heard the voice at the other end, he became alert and apologetic.

'Your Excellency, I was in the toilet.' He lied to appease the big boss.

'First thing first, Doctor. Nature is supreme. You do well.' Mark sounded friendly.

'Thank you, Sir.' Fred was curious to know the reason for a direct contact with the President. 'How is madam responding to treatment Sir?'

'Which of the treatments, Fred?' Mark's voice was high and demanding.'

I don't understand you, Sir.'

'You did, Fred. Why didn't you tell me everything about Maggy?'

Doctor Fred now understood the irritation behind the President's voice. 'It's not my duty to do so, Sir. I didn't want to jump protocol. I was waiting for your physician. It's not what I could discuss on the phone. My conversation with him was on the hemorrhage and the pregnancy of the First Lady.'

'Why did you put it in the record then?'

'I had to, but I did it very professionally because of the personality.'

'You have done well to expose my shame to the world without letting me know first.'

'I am sorry, Your Excellency.'

The President was thoughtful for a while as he thought of what line of action to take next. He knew of the Director of National Hospital's loyalty to the Vice President, his major opposition within the National Party, scheming to take over *Seaview Fortress,* the official residence of Zowambia President. 'Who else knew about what we are talking about?' Mark spoke in a friendly tone.

'I kept the info to myself, Sir.' Fred said impulsively and quickly added, 'the two paramedics that carried out the test knew about the positive result. But I am sure they were only fifty per cent certain who, between the two ladies it belonged to, I did the labelling and identification by myself.

'But you are sure of the result?'

'I am hundred per cent certain, Sir.'

'I will want you and the paramedics to come to London tomorrow with the remaining sample for further tests. You'll be contacted in a moment about your travelling arrangement.' Mark intended to seek their cooperation to be discrete on the ailment.

'We are at your service, Sir.'

'You are at Zowambia's service, Doctor.' Mark smiled and ended the conversation.

xxxxx

President Okuta sent for Idoh and entered the bathroom to get prepared for an unexpected busy night. The doctor was waiting at the room's lobby by the time he emerged from the bathroom. 'You sent for me, Sir.'

'Yeah.' Mark said without looking at him.

'I hope you are okay.' Without waiting for Mark to respond, he added. 'There is some worry in your look. The first lady will be okay. '

'That's not the cause of my concern.'

'What is it, then?'

'I wouldn't want to tell you in order to limit the number of those who know.'

'Whatever it is affects your health. Therefore, I must be in the picture.' Idoh employed the persuasive approach of experience medics. 'Four people are never to be left in the dark in one's affairs, priest in spiritual matters, wife in social matters, doctor in health matters and your attorney in legal matters. I know this is health matter and it is in my jurisdiction. That's why I am employed to make the first family stay healthy.' Idoh stopped and studied the expression on the face of the President as he sat beside him on the sofa. It was an unusual closeness and the doctor knew instinctively that the President had something confidential to discuss. 'I am waiting, Your Excellency. Don't be a difficult patient.' Idoh smiled patronisingly.

'The problem at hand is both social and political. It is thus not within your jurisdiction.' Mark said, almost to himself but Idoh heard.

If such is making you to look like this, I must know the background of the cause of the tension. You know that your heart is not in the best of condition, Mr. President.'

'Do you want to hear it?'

'I am listening, Mr. President.'

'I want to have one more term at Seaview Fortress.'

That's known to everybody, including your ambitious Vice President.'

'Can a HIV-infected family be elected in Zowambia?'

'It's not possible for now.' Idoh replied. 'You'll beat such candidate, silly, at the polls.'

'Then I should forget the next election.'

Idoh was confused. 'Are you saying there is an AIDS patient in the first family?'

The President nodded in the affirmative.

'How come I don't know?' Idoh wondered aloud.

'Maybe you did not do your duty.'

'Mark!' Idoh threw protocol to the wind to address his President. They were friends and classmates in the University. Idoh was no doubt a competent and successful physician but it was their past association that gave him the job in the Presidency. 'Tell me what's going on.'

'I feel reluctant to tell you.' Mark smiled. He knew he could count on friendship if there is the need for Idoh to break professional rule for his sake.

'I will quit the job and concentrate on my private practice if you can't confide in me on health matters.'

'If you do, I'll order the closure of Bibilari Clinic, Presidential order.' Mark smiled.

'I know you won't do anything like that.' As an afterthought Idoh spoke again, 'If you do, I will go back to the classroom.'

'I can make sure none of the Universities here takes you. Besides, your travelling documents will be seized!'

'You are not serious, Mark.'

'Mark is here with you now but it will be the President wielding the powers conferred on and usurped by him.' Mark was almost laughing as Idoh thought he was serious.

'Let's go back to the topic. Tell me what I didn't do.'

'The First Lady, Maggy Okuta tested positive.'

'HIV?' Idoh asked the obvious.

'Is there any other way to hide the dreaded disease?'

'This is serious.'

'You tell me.'

'Two years ago, when both of you got tested, it was negative. Remember the campaign you spearheaded that people should submit themselves for HIV-AIDS tests.'

'That was two years ago. I am talking about today, this moment.'

'Who conducted the test, Doctor Ivy Douglas?'

'No. It was done in Nigeria by Fred.'

'Let me find out more from him on this.' Idoh suggested.

'There is no need to. He's coming to London with the paramedics who conducted the tests.'

'When are they arriving here?'

'They will be here before noon tomorrow.'

'Are you sure of this development, Mr. President?'

'I am.' He gave a wry smile. 'The question that should be agitating your mind is on my own HIV-status. One of us must have brought it to the family. This is scandal, IB. A monumental disgrace. Mr. Fidelity is exposed. It must be my fault. Maggy is a virtuous woman, you and I know, inside out . . . '

'Don't start blaming yourself for what has not been confirmed on you too. Her condition might have been through other means.' Fear crept into the doctor's voice as he spoke.

'That's doubtful.'

'Just stop worrying. We could bury the record using all available means within your power.' Idoh knew exactly what the President wanted. Those who knew about it already must keep the news to themselves.

'Doctor Ivy Douglas said such medical info could not be swept under the carpet. She said that such action or inaction is against professional ethics.'

'That's true. But I will make them know that the survival of a nation is more than ethical nonsense. Zowambia needs Mark and this will be the song to the ears of Ivy, Fred and others in the knowledge of the ailment. This is political, not medical.' The idea of what must be done crept to Idoh's mind. He held his thought hostage and smiled crookedly.

'Thank you, dear friend.' Mark stood up to signify the end of conversation.

Before Idoh slept that night, he made two calls to Zowambia, one to Fred who confirmed the travel arrangement to London, the next morning. The other call went to the group called 'Forward Mark,' the political associates of the President, funded by Idoh Bibilari.

xxxxx

The next day, Doctor Fred Agbamuche and the two paramedics were picked up at the National Hospital by one of the President's chauffeur. It was 6am. They had thirty minutes to make the twenty kilometers journey from Longbridge to Seaview airport where Eagle *3*, the official plane of the Vice President, was warming up, getting ready to take the additional medical hands to London. The limo conveying Fred and others cruised at high speed on the ten kilometers bridge that gave Longbridge, its name. A lorry suddenly emerged from one of the feeder roads that poured traffic unto the bridge at every kilometer stretch, without giving right of way to the limo. In an attempt to prevent running into the lorry, the limo driver slammed on the break. The car somersaulted thrice and a petrol tanker coming from the opposite direction ran over it. There was instant fire outbreak that consumed the limo, the petrol tanker and all occupants of the two vehicles. This was the eyewitness account of the accident that caused the longest and heaviest traffic jam in the history of twin cities of Longbridge and Seaview.

Eagle 3 pilot was the first to know of the accident. He was communicating with the driver when he heard the crash and explosion before the phone went off. He called the presidential helicopter to trace the limo on the express bridge. While the bystanders were still wondering about the identity of the victims, the helicopter pilot was confirming the death of Fred and the two paramedics to Eagle *3*. The Vice-President was promptly informed.

Vice-President Ahmed Mando almost collapsed at the news of the death of the Director of National Hospital. It was a personal loss to him. Fred was his personal physician before his appointment. He influenced his political appointment, and the latter's loyalty to him was not in doubt. The previous weekend, Fred had told him that some scandalous news would rock the Presidency very soon. He assured him that the event would help Ahmed's political advancement. Fred had said he wouldn't explain further until the news erupted from other quarters. Fred wouldn't divulge the news but advised the VP to be patient as some of the dirty linens of his political rivals would soon be washed in full glare of the public. He had been unusually happy then. It was their last conversation when they met during Ahmed's visit to the First Lady at the National Hospital.

With this thought in mind, Ahmed felt shattered at the demise of a dependable ally. It was his duty to tell the president that Doctor Fred would not be able to make the journey to London. He got President Okuta on his direct line.

'Good morning, Ahmed.' The President's voice was cheerful. He had a good night rest after the assurance by Idoh that he would get the cooperation of all involved in her wife's health matters.

'Good morning, Mr. President.' Ahmed had heaved after greeting his boss.

'Is anything wrong? You sounded a bit down.'

'Fred and the two paramedics expected in London today met with a ghastly motor accident on their way to the airport.'

'Try to ensure that they get the best treatment. Don't delegate the assignment.'

'They are dead, Mr. President.' Ahmed said, in a grief cold voice.

'Are you saying all of them died?' Mark was alarmed.

'Yes, they were burnt beyond recognition at kilometer four, on the bridge.'

'It is my fault.' The President felt bad.

'It is not your fault, Sir. They died in the course of their service to their fatherland.'

'How do I explain it to Zowambians? The doctors summoned to provide medical support for the First Lady were killed just like that. The cause of the accident must be investigated.'

'There is no need for that, Mr. President.' Ahmed paused. Their presidential limo ran into a dangerously driven lorry. It is purely a common accident.'

'Try to do the needful and pacify their families.'

'Do we send another team as replacement?'

The question brought the President back to the condition of his wife. 'There is no need for it unless there is still some blood sample of the First Lady in the national hospital.'

Vice President Mando considered this. 'I am not sure but I'll ask the Deputy Director of the Hospital.' Then he wondered aloud. 'Why can't the doctors over there obtain another sample from the patient?'

The President was taken aback, but quickly recovered himself. 'Doctor Ivy Douglas here wants the sample taken immediately after the accident. I am a confused man, Ahmed. I don't want my wife to die. I am yielding to all of their requests, reasonable to me or not.'

'All will be well, Sir.' Ahmed consoled his boss. 'I will find out about the blood sample. If it is still available, you will get it before night fall.'

'Thank you, Mr. Vice President. Consider that I am on leave. You have my permission to carry on all state function while I am away. Maggy needs Mark now more than Zowambia needs him. Besides, you are as capable as Mark, if not more capable.'

'Sir, I wish you tell the electorate this during the next primaries.' Ahmed smiled.

'And thus commit political suicide.' Mark laughed softly.

'No, Sir, it would be viewed as political transparency.'

'I don't know what you are talking about, Mr. Vice President.' He paused. 'All I know is that I will thrash you at the primaries if you decide to vie for the post that is not yet vacant.'

'Let's wait until the primaries, Mr. President. Remember that I am the party man. Let me go for the blood sample.' Ahmed pressed the end mode of his mobile phone.

Mark tried to get to Doctor Bibilari on the phone but there was no response from his room. He called the presidential guard instead. 'Where is the doctor?'

'He is not in the lodge, Sir.' Suara Magaji answered.

'It is just 7:15am.' The President observed.

'He must have gone on his routine check up on Her Excellency. He told me he would be back from the hospital before you wake up.' Suara said, rapidly.

'I need him now.'

'Then, I'll call him to come back immediately.'

'Let him be.' Mark said thoughtfully. 'I need the progress report on Maggy too. Other matters can wait.'

'I'll send him to you immediately he's back.'

'What of the PA?' Mark was referring to his press officer who doubles as his personal assistant.

'Mrs. Pedro is in her room, your Excellency. She had just sent for coffee.'

'Get her to come over and share the coffee with me.' Mark ordered.

'I'll do so immediately.' There was no need to reply as Suara realised the line was off.

The President regarded Labake Pedro more than just a press officer attached to him. She had been very helpful in some political and social decisions made by the President. A highly cerebral widow, an economist turned journalist who had been the toast of all foreign diplomats and journalist that visited the Seaview Fortress. She led the presidential campaign team in the Wam region. Mark had a land slide victory there. He scored hundred per cent votes in the Charanchi, Kankia and Santa-sabo constituencies. After the election, Labake was given the option to choose a ministerial post within the cabinet or manage the foreign office in either USA or Great Britain. The President was surprised when Labake chose to go back to journalism. He wouldn't accept such refusal from an effective organiser to be part of his team. A compromise was reached. She accepted to be the press officer to Mark, a journalist in the corridor of power. To the Zowambians and the world, Labake was a press officer attached to the Presidency. To Mark, Labake was his personal assistant and number one confidant in political and personal matters. Mark needed somebody to talk to and his PA came readily to mind. She might have a better idea on how to handle the HIV palaver.

xxxxx

Mrs. Labake Pedro came into the security office adjoining the president's room and looked curiously at Suara. He understood her questioning look and told her he wouldn't know why the call to her was urgent.

'Go in please, but drop all metal objects on you.' Suara pointed to the steel door leading to the president's suite.

'Do I have to? I am the press officer.'

'You will be alone there with him, madam, in a foreign land. We have to follow protocol. Remember that Brutus betrayed Caesar.'

Labake smiled and dropped her room key and the metal pen she had with her. 'I'll get a pen from him, if need be.'

'Thank you, madam.'

'It's my pleasure.' She smiled and opened the steel door.

Mark had her footsteps and spoke aloud. 'Come into the room, Labake. I am dressed up.'

'Good morning, Your Excellency.' She genuflected to give respect to her boss.

He motioned her to a sofa opposite the one he occupied. 'Help yourself to the coffee.'

As she made two cups of coffee for both of them, Mark told her of the incident reported from Zowambia. He deliberately omitted the HIV status of Maggy.

'What's so important in the blood sample since the donor is here with us? We could simply take another sample from her.' Labake stated.

Mark considered the question. It was first asked by the Vice President. Now his PA asked the same question that would be the million-dollar question on everybody's lip, soon. 'I think the doctors here want to examine the original blood on her before the transfusion of the ones already administered. The blood group thing, you know.' Mark studied the expression on Labake. There was no suspicion in it.

'I see.' She tried to digest the situation from medical angle, too. 'What would Dr Ivy do now?'

'I have asked the VP to check if there's still an extra unit of the blood sample in the lab for Dr Ivy's use.

'I will brief her of the situation when I get to the hospital this morning.' Labake said casually.

'Don't!' The President jumped to his feet. He knew instantly he had over-reacted.

'Why, Mr. President?' Without waiting for an answer, she added, 'after all, the doctor ordered for the sample to be brought.'

The President seemed cornered by his highly intelligent assistant. He decided to open up to his image maker with the press. I sent for the blood sample, not Ivy's order.'

'Why?' Labake looked straight into his eyes. She knew he had something serious on his mind.

'Sit down, next to me, Labake.' When she had done so, he continued. 'I wanted the sample here because it contains scandalous information on the first family. I wanted it destroyed but I ended up destroying innocent souls.'

'I don't understand you, Sir.'

The President smiled. 'I am happy you resisted my having an affair with you. My heart would have been bloodier than it is now if we have had fun. I still remember how you tactically withdrew from my hold in Geneva last weekend.' Mark stopped and looked at her confused press officer.

'You are talking of blood sample and you are going back to something else. It would still happen between us if you find me desirable after you leave office, Mr. President. I love you for your understanding the problems of widows and your efforts to help us. That is enough to make any of us desire your company. But it's not right for any widow to steal what belongs to Maggy. If I allow you now, there won't be a limit. You know I spend more hours of nights and days, put together, with you, than you spend with Her Excellency. I'll rather wait until you are a free citizen to consummate my affection, Mr. President. Then, I would know it wasn't the opportunity of our working relationship alone . . . . '

'It will never happen between us, Labake.' Mark cut in.

'Why are you backing out now?'

'It is because of the blood sample.' Mark managed to say.

'What about it? You are not coherent, Sir. First, it's the blood sample, then your happiness that I refused to give you what I am reserving, on purpose, till a later date. Now the date will never come. Is it because of the blood sample of the First Lady?'

'Yes, Labake.'

'What's in it?' Labake frowned.

'AIDS. Maggy is HIV positive.' The President said, slowly stood up and went to the cabinet for some whisky.

Labake was frozen on her seat. How, why, when. Questions raged in her head. By inference, Mark may be carrying the deadly germ hence his happiness she resisted his moves to have sex with her. He wouldn't want her to share from the virus. It is a sign of true affection and she was grateful to him. She was going to help him, to be by him, whatever comes out of this scandal. She would prove to Mark she is a dependable personal assistant, and a true representative of all Zowambia widows who he had given hope and livelihood.

She stood up from the seat and walked to the President. He was about to sip his drink but her gesture made him stop mid-way. She collected the cup from him and put it on the cabinet. Facing him she rolled her eyes invitingly, closed them and presented her generous lips to Mark, who hesitated and pulled away from her, gently.

'Don't you know there are hundred per cent possibilities that I am infected too?' He managed to say,

'It doesn't matter, Mr. President. I have seen you kissing AIDS-patients. You can't contact HIV through lipial engagement.' She said and moved on him. Before he could protest she had taken the initiative. They kissed actively the way she had never allowed it before. 'The virus is not in saliva according to experts.' She touched his lips with her forefinger.

'I wouldn't believe I was kissing you, Labake. It was so sensuous.'

'I moved on you to remove the noticeable tension on you.' She paused. 'I was preparing my body for the disease too. You need some encouragement, Mr. President.'

'You must be crazy.'

'For you to tell me of your wife's status and express your happiness that we never had fun makes you a real man with heart. I will make love to the man, the heart and not what is in the blood.' She paused, looked at him and closed her eyes. 'Here in London before any test is conducted on you.'

'God forbid.' Mark said,

'Yes, God that forbids some actions of men also allow such actions if they would benefit mankind. Labake approves this.' She was removing her gown when the Presidents hotline came through. It was Idoh Bibilari at the security post. The President was happy at the interruption despite the state of readiness of his body for action. Woman is a complex being, he mused.

Doctor Idoh Bibilari was not surprised to meet the press officer with the President. The closeness of the duo had been a grapevine gist in the presidency. Her secret name among the Presidential entourage and domestic staff was Second Lady. Everyone close to the Presidency, including Idoh, was convinced about the deep relationship between Mark and Labake. The joke was that, she was not just having the ears, the eyes and the head of the President; she was having his body at a higher frequency than Maggy, the first lady.

She was still adjusting her dress when Idoh came in. The doctor inwardly insinuated that he had either interrupted or had come in, to the show, after the closing glee. Idoh suddenly felt pity for Labake. The affliction of the first lady, if it originated from the President, is on her, too. Possibly. He would find a way to subject her to test, later. It might be difficult to ask the President to do the same. Positive result of HIV-test on Mrs. Labake Pedro, would indirectly reaffirm the status of Mark since he sleeps with the two affected ladies, Idoh concluded within himself.

'Good morning, Mr. President. How was the night?'

'Good, IB. How is Maggy?'

'She looks better this morning. She's looking forward to seeing you with the . . .' He stopped as he noticed Mark and Labake exchange a momentary glance, full of meaning that was, however, not communicated to him.

'You wanted to say the blood sample.' Mark completed the hanged sentence for the doctor.

'Yes.' Idoh knew Mrs. Pedro must have been informed. There was no curiosity in her.

'I have briefed Labake. She is the pressman here. It is better for her to be involved from the beginning. It will enable her to manage the situation with the press.'

It was Labake who spoke next. 'I am sure Doctor Bibilari is unaware of the accident in Longbridge.'

'What accident?' Idoh appeared jolted.

'Dr Fred and others are dead. The limo crushed by a trailer on their way to the airport.' Labake narrated the incident, slowly and remorsefully.

Idoh stood fixed. He did not alter a word as others looked on. Mark thought that doctors were all the same. Death is a regular occurrence around them. This accounts for their ability to hide and control their emotional state, even at the death of a loved one.

'The Lord giveth and the Lord taketh. May their soul rest in perfect peace.' Idoh managed to say.

'Amen.' Labake joined.

'Where is the blood sample?' Idoh said, almost to himself.

'It is stupid to ask for the beard of an Immam that got roasted beyond recognition in a fire disaster.' Mark came to Idoh and patted him on the shoulder.

'But we need to be sure.' He spoke in a low voice for the President's ear alone.

'To be sure of what?'

'That the blood sample, all of it, is no more in National Hospital. And the record, too.'

'I understand the doctor, Mr. President.' Labake spoke. 'You were thinking of re-conducting the test in London while the doctor wanted the evidence destroyed in order to cover-up the eventual scandal.'

'You are right.' Idoh agreed.

'Then I hope the deaths of Fred and the paramedics were purely accidental.' Mark was deep in thought as he realised he wanted the blood sample destroyed, too. He was not happy that the doctors met with the same fate. He did not wish them dead.

'That's my fear too.' Idoh said. 'Who knows whether Fred had talked to somebody in the opposition? Who knows if the first lady's blood sample and test result are in the hands of an enemy? Who knows if such people eyeing the presidency had arranged his death? Who knows what really happened in Longbrigde? Who can assure us that all is well? Who—'

'Don't get hysteric IB.' Mark stopped his friend's musings. 'I have ordered the VP to check if there is still Maggy's blood sample at the National hospital—'

'So that he can take it and use it against you?' Idoh cut in.

'He doesn't know anything about the blood, IB.'

'Supposing Fred mentioned it to him. You know the late doctor is more loyal to him. The VP gave him the job.'

'It is possible.' Labake chipped in.

'Alright, alright.' Mark put up both hands. 'Let the story unfold on its own. We shall cross the bridge when we get to the river.'

'The President might be lucky to avoid a scandal from this.' Labake smiled and moved in such a way that stirs desire in both men watching her. 'Without sounding callous, the death of Fred and his crew had eliminated the available evidence of the scandal. We shall be very lucky if Doctor Ivy is the only person who knew about the result of the test. She could be talked to silence.' She suggested

'I hope so.' Mark considered his discussion with Doctor Ivy Douglas, the previous night at Embassy Hospital.

The security officer called to announce the arrival of the President of Ashanti and his wife at the reception of Zowambia Lodge. Idoh withdrew to his room as the President, accompanied by his press officer, moved down the corridor to meet President and Lady Gilbert Osaigbovo.

xxxxx

Idoh Bibilari got to Embassy Hospital at noon to meet Doctor Douglas as pre-arranged.

'She is looking better.' Idoh posted. 'I came in earlier to see her.'

'There is no more danger. Her system accepted the blood perfectly.'

'Our doctors are good, Ivy. It's only we still have that mentality of obtaining the best medical treatment abroad.'

'There is no doubt about that.' Ivy smiled, 'judging from how Doctor Fred handled the treatments so far.'

'He is the head of the National Hospital.'

'Ivy frowned in thought. 'There was a bad news about your National Hospital on the BBC this morning.'

'What's it?' Idoh waited expectantly for the obvious.

'A limo containing three doctors from the National Hospital on an unspecified assignment was crushed in an accident. No survivor.'

'That's serious.' Idoh feigned ignorance of the news.

'The accident led to the heaviest traffic jam in the history of Longbridge. The confusion was shown briefly on the cable network.'

'Were the names of the doctors involved mentioned?

'A name was mentioned. It didn't sound like Fred's but it was said that the National Hospital's director was involved.'

'It couldn't be.' Idoh pretended to be alarmed. 'If it is so, Longbridge will be in serious confusion now.'

'In fact, I was banking on the President's promise to invite him over for re-examination of the First Lady.' She deliberately left the word blood out of the sentence.

'The President will not like this.' Idoh said, pensively.

'I don't like it either. it means I will have to start the examination on the First Lady, all over.'

'I will assist you.' Idoh offered himself.

'Thanks, doctor.'

'I'll arrange for her blood sample before the day is over.' Ivy looked up as she saw President Mark Okuta approaching from the hallway. 'Here comes His Excellency.'

They exchanged greetings and Ivy led the President, Idoh and Labake to the bedside of Lady Maggy Okuta.

Maggy attempted to sit up on the bed but Ivy motioned her not to do so. She smiled as her husband bent down to kiss her. Her face was warm and glowing with affection despite her condition. His kiss was equally warm, more so when he realised that Maggy held on to his lips and briefly expressed with her tongue how she had missed him.

'I could see you are getting better, my lady.' The President was happy at her recovery progress.

'I feel better now. At least I know who I am and where I am. It is unlike how I felt a few days ago.'

'Who are you?' Mark asked her, smiling.'

'I am Mark's wife.'

'Who is Mark?'

'The son of Okuta who had a demanding kiss from me just now.'

Everyone present, including Ivy, could not help but laugh at the exchanges between the President and the First Lady. Their daily life was characterized by such banters. They had a simple and principled domestic life. Outside the paraphernalia of office, Mark would always want to be seen as an ordinary man, son to a peasant farmer and the wife had imbibed his simple philosophy of living. They were not power drunk; there was no delusion of grandeur characteristic of many African leaders. Mark knew that Zowambia was a unique country. Presidency was not the birth-right of any individual. You had to do well to win a second term in office. And failure to win a second term was regarded as a failure of governance during the first term. Zowambians called it a necessary surgery to the system. Despite the fact that Mark and Maggy were not obsessed with power, they loved to go for a second term. They wanted to consolidate on their first term which they had evaluated themselves with average performance. They knew that their praise singers, hangers-on, political jobbers and party machinery that scored them very high were doing so for selfish reasons. Mark wanted to leave something concrete for posterity and he firmly believed that a second term would give him the opportunity to make the difference in Zowambia.

'The President of Ashanti and his wife sent their greetings. They stopped over this morning to see you.' Mark was alone with his wife. Others had withdrawn to allow husband and wife some privacy.

'That's nice of the couple.' Maggy smiled again and tried to hide a sharp pain she experienced in her neck region as she spoke. 'I want us to emulate that great couple by doing something concrete for Zowambia. We must leave behind an enviable legacy in political and economic developments.'

'That's if we have the opportunity to stay at Seaview Fortress after November.' Mark reminded her of the coming election.

'I don't have any doubt that you are going to win. You are always a winner, an achiever, a go-getter. The record is there. The good we have done outweigh the bad. I think the only bad or ugly deed of your administration is allowing the hawks, those men who have looted the treasury in the past to hold sway in your cabinet.' Maggy stated, objectively.

Mark nodded in agreement. 'Those greedy party-men were in the ZNP before me. My hands were tied then.'

'Remove the strings in your hand during your second coming and be Mark Okuta.' Maggy said encouragingly.

'That's my woman.' He sat on the bed, bent down and kissed her again. This time, she slid in her tongue and searched, frantically in the mouth cavity of her husband for the medicine to remove her pains and calm the rising waves.

'I learnt that you are pregnant, too.' Mark told her after the kiss.

'It is not yet confirmed.' She wasn't surprised to hear it from the husband. 'I told Doctor IB that I missed my period. I don't want to raise our hope until he confirms the pregnancy as well as the gender of the baby.'

'You don't need to worry, Maggy. I am alright with the three girls.'

'I want to have your son.'

'Do I need one? Did I tell you I am desperate to have one?'

'But you are a man, an African, all African men desire male offspring.'

'If they can't get it, what do they do?'

"'They look for other women who will give it to them.' Maggy snapped. 'Or women look for them with such an offer. We have witnessed both categories. Yours won't be any different.'

'Maggy,' the President spoke gently and affectionately, 'Don't get desperate to satisfy me on this issue of a male-child. I am okay with my girls. I have three. Bill Clinton of America had one. They were a happy family before, during and after their occupation of White House. Let's be contended with what we have, darling.'

'I agree with you.' Maggy soft-pedalled on her drive. 'But if I am truly pregnant and it is a male child, it will be a welcome addition.'

'What of if it came out a female child again?'

'I won't like to carry such for nine months.'

'I won't allow you to abort my baby, whichever the sex.' Mark voice was serious and Maggie knew it.

'That's alright.' Maggy kissed him lightly to calm him down.

'It will be a miracle if the baby is still there despite all the blood that came out of you.'

'My God is a God of miracles.' She smiled and felt her stomach.

The President then briefed her on everything that had happened, everything minus the blood test that revealed her HIV-status.

'It is a pity Doctor Fred died. He saved my life and lost his.' Maggy felt guilty. 'When I have my boy, he's going to take his name, Fred, as a honour to him. Mark Fred Okuta. That's my boy's name.'

'What is the name if it came out a girl?'

'I will name her Freda.'

'You are so sentimental. That's one of your strong and weak points, darling.' Mark got off the bed as there was a knock on the door. It was the protocol officer to the President who came in to remind him of the appointment he scheduled for Zowambia Embassy in London for the next hour.

xxxxx

Negro Restaurant was in East London. It was very popular for its African dishes and Idoh had formed the habit of visiting the joint anytime he came to London. He would like to go there this evening. The thought was on his mind during the evening round at the Embassy Hospital. As the two nurses were leaving, tired-looking Ivy entered Lady Maggy Okuta's room. Maggy was already dosing off. It was two days earlier they agreed to re-examine Maggy's blood.

'Here you are, Ivy.' Doctor Idoh said. 'You look tired.'

'It has been work all day.' She agreed.

'Then you must come with me to Negro restaurant. They have energizing as well as appetizing dishes.' Idoh gave a boyish smile.

'That's kind of you, but—'

'There is no but.' Idoh cut in. 'The menu is good, the atmosphere is nice. It will be like a father and daughter at dinner apart from our skins. The atmosphere will allow us to discuss more on the other health problem of the First Lady.'

The last part of the patronising words got the best of Ivy. 'I will like to come because of the professional discussion.'

'That's good.'

She looked at the time. 'If we have to, you'll give me some time to keep an appointment before the dinner.

'You are free to, my dear.' Idoh agreed.

'When do I meet you there?'

I intend to send a driver to you or come for you, personally.'

'That won't be necessary. My appointment is in that neighbourhood.' She paused to think. 'I can meet you there at nine if that's not too late.'

'The time suits me.'

Ivy Douglas checked the folder at the foot of the bed, made some remarks and left Idoh with the sleepy First Lady.

Idoh stood up as soon as Ivy closed the door, looked closely at Maggy to ensure she was okay, and re-adjusted his tie in readiness to step out.

'Enjoy your date, doctor.' Maggy said clearly, smiled with eyes firmly closed.

Idoh came back to the bedside. 'So, you are not off yet?'

'How can I be off when there is romantic talk in the air between two friends who wanted to discuss my health problem over dinner?' She waved him goodbye.

Idoh knew he had other reasons, a professional one inclusive, for the invitation to dinner. Let the First Lady imagine romance, he thought as he left the room.

They arrived at the restaurant almost at the same time. A few of the service hands knew Idoh and the duo were promptly attended to. They had a sumptuous dinner. Ivy enjoyed the African spices and Idoh ensured that she had plenty of it. They drank coffee after the meal and spent the rest of the evening discussing the health problem of Lady Maggy Okuta.

'You are already aware of the HIV status of the First Lady.' Ivy opened the discussion.

'Yes. The President told me. I didn't see the report from Nigeria before it got to you.' Idoh responded.

'If you had, you wouldn't have allowed the report.' She put her coffee down and looked straight into the eyes of Idoh.

Idoh considered what to say. He recollected what the President told him about their discussion on the topic.

'You are right, Ivy.'

'That would have been unethical, a gross professional misconduct.' She said, sternly.

'That is true.' He leaned forward to get closer to her. 'In politics, many things do happen. Even here, in Britain. The State takes precedence over work ethics. Yes, it is not good to expose whoever handles her case to the danger. Yes, it is necessary to commence treatment immediately. But we would like it to be a secret because of the political and social scandal to the personalities involved.' Idoh stopped to examine her comprehension of the situation.

'I understand your position and that of the President on this but I won't wait for more than seventy two hours to report the case to the AIDS centre immediately I am hundred per cent certain.' Ivy stated as a matter of fact.

'Let's take the test together again and wait for the result.'

'I have carried out another test.'

'When did you do that?'

'Two hours after she was admitted, three days ago.'

'What's the result?' Idoh knew Ivy only wanted to know if he consented to having another test the last time they discussed.

'Dr. Fred was right. Your First Lady is HIV positive.'

'Did you reconfirm this to the President?'

'Not yet. He didn't want it mentioned. If I were a Zowambian, he would probably arrest me for conducting the test again.'

'Where is the report . . . ?'

'I kept it discretely in my office. That's why I wasn't bothered when the husband took the report from Nigeria. I'll go to the medical director with it tomorrow.'

'I can't stop you, Ivy. You are protecting your job and I am trying to make you bend the rule to protect mine.' He paused. 'The President will talk to your boss on the necessary thing to do or say on the matter.'

'That would be their cup of tea. We are already drinking ours.' She joked.

'We need to wash it down with their special wine, brewed in Africa. Zowambia pride.' Idoh called the waiter and whispered to him.

'That will be fine. I have had about the wine. Black Palmy. A brand of wine that is black in name but white in appearance. I hope it tastes good.'

'Black and white is the best combination of contrasting colours in the world. It is a bitter sweet combination, the devil and the angel. It helps to relax the muscles and one could sleep off in less than an hour after drinking it.'

'It is therefore a bed-time drink.' Ivy remarked as the black wine cups got to their table. 'That's why it is served after dinner in a special glass with the inscription there. Read it.' He pointed to the glass cup in which the wine was served.

'Good night rest.' Ivy read it. She took her glass and they toasted to the good health of the First Lady before gulping it down their throats.

Ivy stood up. 'Thank you, Doctor. I think I'd better go before the wine start working.'

Idoh stood up too. 'It is all exaggeration and a ploy to make more money by the owners of Negro.' He took the bill and paid the waiter.

Outside, the breeze was cool and refreshing. The moon was up and the clouds were rushing over it in quantum. Ivy turned to the older doctor, gave him a peck on the chick and entered into her car. As she drove off, Idoh Bibilari smiled and waved. His hand was still caressing the open void when the diplomatic driver attached to him brought him back to the present. He jumped inside and directed the driver to Embassy Hospital.

xxxxx

The next morning, President Mark Okuta came to the hospital very early to bid his wife farewell. He needed to go back to Zowambia to attend to an urgent security matter in the oil-producing area of Biam region. The nation's wealth was from crude-oil export and any disruption to the exploration and mining normally got the utmost attention from the President. He had been successful in this area, more than his predecessors. He wouldn't want the record reversed at this twilight stage of his first term in office.

'Let me have a word with Doctor Douglas.' Mark spoke to the nurse attending to his wife.

'She is yet to come this morning.'

'Is she on afternoon duty?' Mark probed further. He would like to extract some reassurance from Ivy on the matter they earlier discussed.

The nurse responded. 'She is two hours late, already and that's unusual of her. She combined morning and afternoon duties, yesterday, and she ought to have called if she wasn't fit to report to work.'

The President considered this. 'Maybe IB will stay behind until the doctor comes.'

Idoh came alive at the mention of his name by his boss. His mind had wondered off to the wonderful dinner he had with Ivy the previous night. 'I was here in the night yesterday on a routine check on the First Lady. One of the patients was gasping and the nurse tried Ivy on the phone. The phone rang out several times. One would assume she was deeply asleep then.' Idoh paused. 'But for her not to be at work now probably means she wasn't home. Have you called her this morning?'

'Several times with no responses,' the nurse said, 'and the phone rang out on each occasion.'

'You ought to have sent somebody to find out.' Idoh remarked.

'There is no condition serious enough to warrant the effort.'

'What of Mr. President waiting to see her?'

'We could call the police to check on her, then.'

'Please, do.' Idoh pleaded with a patronising smile.

There was no need to do so. As the hospital attendant was going to the front desk to make the call, two policemen were already reporting the death of Ivy Douglas at the hospital's security post. She was found stone dead inside her bathtub. According to an initial police report, she didn't finish her bath before a suspected cardiac struck. There was no break-in or foul play suspected. She must have died of exhaustion.

There was atmosphere of uncertainty in the hospital as Ivy's death was instantly relayed to all departments. President Mark Okuta was restricted to his wife's room by his security aides. Idoh and Labake stood there with him, both dumbfounded. Maggy heard what happened and when her eyes, full of questions, met Idoh's, the latter shook his head in a manner that told her he didn't know anything about the incident.

It was the President who broke the enveloping silence when there was no stranger in the room. 'I am beginning to have my doubt about the death of Fred in Zowambia. It may not be an accident, after all.' Mark paused. 'With Ivy's death, I hope my wife won't be given a bad name. Doctor Killer.'

Nobody could respond for a while to the dry fact of two deaths in a row. 'I am beginning to suspect the two were murdered.' Labake Pedro found her voice.

'What could have been the murderer's motive?' Maggy spoke as she managed a sitting position on her sick-bed.

'If it is a murder, then the perpetrator is after me. My enemies want to destroy my political career, using my wife's hospitalisation to start this serial killing.' Mark looked at Idoh and Labake. 'We don't need to discuss this further in the presence of Maggy. She must not be allowed to have an emotional trauma.'

The two understood the President's real reason for wanting to end the discussion. They knew that the only information that late Fred and Ivy had was the HIV-status of Maggy. The President summoned them out of the room and closed the door, leaving Maggy alone on her hospital bed.

'I hope none of us is doing this.' Mark looked from Labake to Idoh. They looked back straight at him and shook their head.

'Yes, my wife is HIV-positive and by association, I am likely to be an AIDS-victim, too. That's personal scandal. It is not a crime but a social stigma. Murder is a serious crime that could lead to death sentence or life imprisonment. I am telling you here that I don't intend to silence those who knew about my wife HIV-condition by killing them. I wanted to persuade them to help me keep my secret for a while. Who knows how many individuals know about her ailment now? I am beginning to fear these deaths may lead to a greater international scandal for me. I don't want to run for a second term at all cost. Whether these killings were an inside job or by my enemies, they will not do my administration any good. Right now, I do not want to hide the problem any more. I'll face it and get myself tested too. By the time our dear Maggy knows that I am also a victim, she will be able to bear her cross.' Mark stopped and smiled to ease the tension, he had built with his speech.

'There is still fifty-fifty chance that the deaths are accidental or natural.' Labake spoke softly. 'Don't let us attract any suspicion on our First Lady.'

The President coughed as he was about to speak. When the action stopped, he wiped his face with the back of his hand. 'I could feel some heat inside me as a result of this. I'll postpone my departure until afternoon in order to know to which extent Ivy's death will be linked to her work in the hospital.'

'That's a good decision, Mr. President.' Idoh liked Mark's postponing his journey.

'And the earlier arrangement that Doctor Bibilari stay behind is still unchanged.' Labake faced Idoh. 'It is important he stays behind to get acquainted with the new doctor that will be assigned to the First Lady.'

'It is my duty and honour.' Idoh said. 'And I have a feeling that we won't have to worry anymore about the HIV thing. Our concern will be how to take care of the First Lady on arrival in Nigeria.'

'You are obsessed with this second term thing, Doctor.' Labake said jokingly.

'It is on course.'

'I don't understand your enthusiasm, IB.' Mark injected.

'Simple.' He responded. 'I need a promotion from personal physician to Minister of Health. We need to make any move necessary to take us there.' Idoh revealed his interest in ministerial appointment.

'Don't make murderous moves, please.' Mark said, looking at the direction of his wife's hospital room.

'I am talking about political moves, not murder, Mr. President.' Idoh smiled as the president and his press officer walked back to Maggy's room.

Idoh decided to visit the nurse's room. He would see Maggy later, alone. He would let her know it was only dinner he had with Ivy, nothing else.

The nurses were making arrangement to brief the replacement of the late Ivy Douglas when Idoh entered.

'We couldn't find the original medical file for the Zowambia First Lady.' One of the nurses, who knew him as the family's personal physician, spoke.

'Check the patient's bed-foot.' Idoh was sure it was not there but knew it was where the folder ought to be.

'It is not there.' Two nurses responded together.

'Then, check Ivy's office or the medical director's office.'

The nurse agreed with him. One of them left the room to look for the record. Idoh smiled for his thoughtfulness. During the previous night, he had brought another copy of the medical report of Maggy, supposedly recorded by Dr Fred Agbamuche, to the small office of Ivy. Only this time there was no reference to the HIV test or result there from. He had frantically searched for the new test recorded by Ivy but failed to locate it. There was no time to check everywhere then. It was an unauthorised entry. He had planned to use the changed medical report he now directed the nurse to pick as his object of search, if caught. He had left the forged document there out of panic as he heard movement towards his direction, then. Idoh was inwardly pleased with himself for his zealous attitude to cover the scandal for his boss. The disappearance of the folder would have been linked to the death of Ivy. Zowambia would have been number one suspect for murder.

Instantly, Idoh followed the nurse to Ivy's office. The folder was on the table where he left it. 'Oh! You have found it.'

'Yes. Thank you,' said the unsuspecting nurse. 'The new doctor will need it.'

As she talked he took a sweeping look at the small room. It was only the small bookshelf that contained about a dozen medical journals that he did not check the previous night. One of the journals with the inscription 'Malaria: Deadlier than HIV-AIDS' attracted him. He picked the volume. 'I have not read this.'

The nurse looked at the journal. 'Me, either. It is on malaria, an African scourge. Not common here. It is a tropic affair and problem.'

'You are right, my dear.' Idoh tried to be friendly. 'Let me go through it while I am with the First Lady. It will keep me busy while waiting on her majesty.

The nurse seemed to be confused on whether to allow him or not. Borrowing her book out for a few hours was no crime. She considered the fact that Ivy was dead. The man could have it. 'Make sure you hand it over to me before you go.' She finally conceded after what seemed a long silence of hesitation to Idoh.

'Thank you. I'll return it in an hour.'

Idoh left with the book while the nurse took the fake medical report as the one from Zowambia.

xxxxx

Idoh met the President at the door of Maggy's room. The President was going back to the Villa in preparation for his journey back to Zowambia.

'Am I staying back in London as suggested earlier?' Idoh asked the President as the latter pulled him to a corner for what seemed to be a private discussion. Labake and the security personnel's in the entourage stayed at a respectable distance from them.

'Maggy told me that the late doctor took about a pint of her blood and explained to her she wanted to do some analysis on it.' Mark informed him, ignoring his question.

'I know, Mr. President.' Idoh smiled to ease the tension on Mark's face.

'Then, she must have conducted her own HIV-test.'

'She had, and the test was positive.'

'Now that she's dead, whoever conducted the test for her would definitely know that my wife is . . . '

'She was discrete about it,' he paused as he realised he cut in without allowing the President to finish. When he was sure Mark was not continuing, he added, 'And she had poured away the remaining blood sample.'

'How did you know this?'

'She told me yesterday.'

'And you didn't think I should know about it.'

'I do not want to make you panic.'

'I need to know.' Mark's voice was reprimanding.

'I am sorry, Mr. President.' Idoh paused and moved closer to Mark. 'Since I knew about the existence of another positive result, I have been trying to get hold of it. I wanted to get it before I tell you.'

'You didn't ask for her permission?'

'She is not alive to grant such a request. I am the most qualified to have the info.'

'I see.' Mark was thinking. 'If any detective finds out you are keen on taking her record without permission since last night, you will be number one suspect for her murder.' Mark looked at his time. It was almost 12noon.

'No detective knew about the last blood sample and test yet.'

'What of Detective Mark Okuta? I am interested in finding out what killed Doctor Ivy. She was so full of life.'

'The autopsy will give us the clue.'

'I don't believe in autopsy conclusions. It is a mere academic exercise in medical jargons. There had been cases where autopsy gave the cardiac arrest as the reason for death, but later the person who applied poison owned up as the murderer.'

'You are right, Mr. President.'

'Good luck, if you get the record, IB. But, I really don't care any more if the result is made public. I have a feeling that our opponents masterminded the deaths of Fred and Ivy. I have a feeling that further attempts by us to conceal the record may lead to more deaths, death of any doctor that handles her case.

'I still want to believe that the deaths are coincidental to, not as a result of, the positive test.' Idoh spoke with conviction. 'I'll still go ahead and get the new record. It must be somewhere in that room.'

'I am not interested. You are neither a detective nor a thief but you are Idoh Bibilari, my friend and family doctor. I will disown you and deny the knowledge of what you are doing if you are caught doing something unexplainable.'

'I understand you, Mark.'

'Good. Try to take care of my wife. That's your primary assignment here.' The President walked briskly to Labake and others.

Idoh stood there watching them disappear behind the entrance glass door. He turned his attention to the book on malaria. He observed there was an envelope kept in the inner folder of the back cover. He brought it out. The sealed envelope was marked 'ZFL—personal.' The hand writing was definitely Ivy's. ZFL. Idoh spelt the letters out to himself many times. What could those letters stand for? Zowambia file? It may have something to do with Zowambia, with Lady Maggy's illness. Yes ZFL. Zowambia First Lady. That must be it. He looked at the manila envelope all over again. He decides to put it away in the inner pocket of his jacket. The owner would not miss it. The owner is dead. He had the strongest feeling that the envelope contained the result of the blood test of Zowambia First Lady, ZFL.

A nurse who walked past him and entered Maggy's room brought Idoh back from his reverie. He decided to go to the toilet while the nurse was still busy with Maggy. In the privacy of the toilet, he sat comfortably on the loo and tore open the envelope. The content confirmed his guess and suspicion. The First Lady is not only HIV-positive, she is also pregnant and the baby carries the risk of infection.'

'The President must know this immediately.' He said to himself as he folded back the paper and tucked it into his pocket. He tried the President's private number and there was response at the first burr.

'What is it, Doctor?' Mark was curious to know why Idoh called barely two minutes after he departed from him. 'Is anything wrong with Maggy?'

'Maggy is okay, Mr. President.' Idoh paused. 'There is something you must know.'

'What?' Mark's eagerness increased.

'I have what we are looking for. It was there in my hand when we met at the door but I didn't know.' Idoh stopped to confirm if the President understood him.

'Are you sure?'

'Yes. It included something else, too.'

'Are you with Maggy?'

'No, Sir.'

'I don't want her to know about her status yet. I want to postpone her reaction to my unfaithfulness and her predicament until she is completely strong to withstand the shock.'

'Don't blame yourself, Mark the Saint.' Idoh seldom called the President by his school nickname. As a friend, he has the liberty to level up with the President and he thought Mark needed a friendly advice on the issue. 'You are only human, not the saint. It might not be your fault. The ailment comes through various media. Hers may have been through such media.'

'What other media?' Mark voice was not cheerful. He didn't believe that he was not the cause of Maggy's problem.

'It can't be discussed on the phone.'

'Then come over to the Villa.' Mark commanded. 'I still have a few hours before the flight back home.

'I'll do so right away after seeing the First Lady.' Idoh came out of the toilet and saw the nurse coming out of Maggy's room.

Maggy was expecting him. She hardly allowed him to close the door before she talked. 'I thought you are avoiding me.' She said aloud.

'Why would I do that?' Idoh knew what was going to follow. 'If it was my date with late Ivy, I am innocent of what happened to her. We had dinner and parted ways from the restaurant.'

'I thought you engaged her in all night duty.' Maggy cut in, and looked at Idoh who tried to avoid her probing eyes. 'We've heard of cases of cardiac arrest after bouts of sex.'

'We only had dinner, and nothing else.' Idoh stated again.

'From the manners in which the invitation was given and accepted, I wanted to believe the Negro outing would go beyond professional dinner.' Maggy smiled. She looked healthier than the previous day.

'It was strictly professional.' Idoh said thoughtfully. 'Intimacy or sex didn't cross my mind for a second while we were together. We only discussed your health.'

'Why didn't you tell your friend that you had dinner with her yesterday night?'

'I don't want to be seen as a suspect to murder.'

'Don't you think somebody else know of your dinner date?'

'Yes.' Idoh thought for a while. 'Many people saw me with her in the restaurant.'

Maggy asked him so sit closer to her. 'If you don't know anything about her death, it is better you let the hospital's director know you had dinner with her last night.' She said slowly.

'What will be the use for that?'

She smiled. 'If the autopsy confirms murder, then you'll be suspect number one. Your failure to mention it and the eventual knowledge of your outing through investigation will send you to jail, pronto. The damage will have been done to your name, to Zowambia image before the truth is known.'

'You are right.' Idoh agreed. Even Mr. President would almost believe that I killed her. I did not mention to him that I took Ivy to Negro restaurant.'

'I wondered why you kept silent on it. If you are not our doctor and friend, I would have called the police when the news of the death got to us. You looked indifferent. I could not see the shock expected from a close acquaintance that was with you before she went home and died or got killed.'

'You suspected me.'

I did. But now, having heard you that there was no love tangle after dinner, my mind is clear about your innocence.' Maggy said, genuinely.

'Thank you, Maggy. It is better I talk to the medical director about yesterday night.'

'Please do. It is equally necessary that Mark knows about it, too.' She watched him approach the door, eager to go out. 'Don't be such in a hurry to do that.'

Let me do so immediately and come back to give Her Excellency a full medical attention.'

The First Lady smiled. 'I am not your patient here.'

'But your Doctor is dead. Until another one is appointed. I'll be in charge.' Idoh paused. 'I am always in charge.'

Maggy always enjoyed his enthusiasm at work. He had been the family doctor for three and half years. They had been good friends in their University days. He had been a lovely gentleman then, He wasn't the type that would take a woman to bed on a first date. Nowadays, he had little or no time for his private practice but seemed happy to serve his friend and nation. She remembered the dialogue between him and Mark on the day of Mark's inauguration.

'You must come to Seaview Fortress as number one doctor in the Presidency.' Mark had said to Idoh, then.

'I'll consider it Mark. Oh I want to say Mr. President.' Idoh realized Mark Okuta was no more an ordinary citizen. He had become the President of Zowambia.

'Quit that protocol, IB, accept my offer and let us serve the nation together.

'I'll consider the offer.' Idoh repeated.

'Take it for the sake of the nation and for friendship.'

'I'll do it for friendship. I lost faith in Zowambia when I was refused scholarship to study medicine. I'll do it for you, Mark Saint Okuta.'

She remembered that they had both laughed as Idoh recalled during that memorable day, Mark's nickname in the high school. The Saint.

'How are you, today?' Idoh spoke again to bring Maggy back to the present.

'I would have been fine, if not for the news about Doctor Ivy.'

'Don't let that disturb your health.'

'She was conducting a test on my blood sample in addition to a pregnancy test.' The First Lady stated, and continued. 'I want you to find out the result of those tests.'

'I'll do so.' Idoh assured her. He was surprised Ivy had mentioned the tests to her.

'Now that I am living on donated blood, I want to know the state of the oil in my heart.' Maggy put her hand on her chest.

'There's no problem, I assure you.'

'Assure me with evidence, doctor. Get hold of that result and let me see it. I want to be hale and hearty for my husband and for the second term activities.'

'You already are.' Idoh walked back to the door, and was out before Maggy could respond again.

He was eager to carry out the suggestion of Maggy on the need to let the director of Embassy Hospital know about his dinner with the late doctor, Ivy Douglas.

xxxxx

Vice President Ahmed Mando had just ended his call to the President when Doctor Idoh Bibilari was ushered in to see the President. Ahmed had just confirmed that there was no more blood sample of both Maggy and her counterpart from Ashanti in the national hospital. The late doctor Fred had collected the whole sample and the file in the test laboratory the night preceding his death in the auto crash. The President had genuinely regretted his decision to ask Fred to come to London with the sample. Ahmed had consoled his boss and told him that the families of the three victims had been visited and assured of government support and compensation for the loss.

'I can confidently tell you that no blood sample of Maggy remained in Zowambia. All burnt in the auto crash.' Mark told the doctor, as the latter took his seat.

'That's good news.' Idoh smiled. 'I am also in possession of the only record of the latest test conducted by Ivy Douglas.'

'You told me that on the phone'. Mark was expectant of the other news.

'Your wife is confirmed pregnant. Her urine test and . . . '

'We don't need another baby.' Mark said coldly. 'Yes I like to have a boy. But I don't want a HIV-positive child. I am not a doctor but I know that the risk of that unborn child being infected is high.'

'I know Mr. President is always against abortion.' Idoh reminded his friend.

'I think there's going to be an exception, doctor.'

'Your wish is my command.' Idoh was thoughtful. 'How do we convince Maggy, more so if the baby is a boy?'

'That's your duty, doctor. If I were you, I wouldn't wait for a scan to determine the sex of the baby before it is flushed out.' Mark advised.

There was silence between them as Mark considered his yet to be determined HIV-status and Idoh considered how to tell the President about himself and Ivy.

'Any other thing you want to tell me?' The President's question almost threw Idoh off his outward calmness.

'I ought to have told you this earlier, Mark. I was with Ivy at Negro restaurant, last night.' Idoh said in an apologetic mood.

'I know you had dinner together but you did not follow her to her residence.'

'You know that?'

'I know more. You went back to the hospital afterwards. And I know you didn't go to Maggy. What were you doing that late in the hospital?'

'Looking for this?' Idoh raised up the result of Maggy's blood test. 'She told me over dinner of a new test she had already conducted on the First Lady and her intention to make it known to the director despite assuring you of her cooperation for a few more days.'

'Is that why you killed her?' The President's voice was cold and casual.

Idoh jumped up from his seat. 'Mark! What did you just say? I am a doctor, not a murderer. I was trained to save live, not to take it. If you were not my friend and my President, I would have headed for the court.'

'My question is not answered yet.' Mark repeated it. 'Why did you kill her?'

'I didn't kill her. I had dinner with her and I have told the hospital's director.'

'I am only preparing you for the interrogation that will come up if the autopsy revealed a foul play or rape.'

'I neither killed nor abused her sexually.'

'That envelope should not be found on you.' Mark stressed his hand and Idoh placed the test result in it. 'I had a feeling I should wait for one more day in London. I have a feeling you are getting too much involved in covering this scandal for my sake. I don't like the coincidences. They are enough clues to put us in trouble.'

Idoh remained seated and silent as the President read through the medical test. Without speaking to Idoh, he stood up and ignited a lighter. The paper and envelope were burnt to ashes and Mark gathered the ashes and flushed them in the toilet.

Idoh knew the President was afraid. He wouldn't want Zowambia to be suspected of any involvement in the murder of Ivy Douglas whenever the truth of the HIV-status of Maggy became known.

'We hope that the last evidence of the truth inside Maggy's blood is down there in the soak-away.' Mark said as he came out of the toilet.

'I am sure there won't be any scandalous information for the oppositions to your second term bid to use against you. You are free to run, Mr. President.'

'Am I free?'

'Of course, you are.'

'Does concealment of the truth make the truth a falsehood, IB? Does the ignorance of Zowambia on the HIV-status of Maggy make Mark and Maggy free from the deadly virus? I am a victim of my own wantonness, my own indiscipline. I am so guilty for Maggy's condition. When we get back home, I must conduct a test to confirm my own status.'

'What use will that serve?'

'It will enable me and my wife to console each other publicly or keep our status strictly to myself without Maggy knowing.'

'You don't need a test, Mr. President. I will put your wife on treatment and her pregnancy will be an excuse for you to avoid with her, meanwhile.'

'That excuse won't work.' Mark knew his wife. 'Besides, I have told you the pregnancy has to go.' Mark took up his phone and called in Labake Pedro. It was his usual way to indicate that the discussion had ended.

Idoh stood up and met the press officer at the door. They exchanged pleasantries and a friendly smile came from Idoh as he took his exit.

The President was lost in thought as Labake took her seat. On several occasions, he had been unfaithful to his wife. He had taken many women to bed before he became President. Almost all the affairs had been arranged either by his trusted officials or personal contacts. His affairs since he became President had not been many. It was difficult to ascertain where he must have contacted the infection he passed on to his wife. He had not allowed passion to override his sense in recent times. He had not engaged himself in naked exposure.

Before now, he had thought that the condom option of the ways to prevent AIDS was most effective. He recollected that during the last four years, he had presented himself for HIV-test on two different occasions. The first time he did it in order to boost his electoral campaign. He had tested negative and the whole world applauded his exemplary leadership, direction and encouragement to get rid of the scourge in Zowambia and Africa. He equally recollected it was over two years ago when Maggy and himself tested negative again. It was at the beginning of the national campaign for prevention of AIDS, initiated by Maggy. He did it to encourage mass participation. The test scared Zowambians more than death itself. He smiled at the recollection of congratulatory messages from other African first ladies who confessed to Maggy that they were afraid to go for HIV-test until her bold step was made public. Now, within the last two years, Mark believed he had contacted HIV through lust and indiscipline. His head was too cloudy and crowded to analyse his very few female contacts. One particular affair he had about a year earlier kept crawling into his memory. It was during an invitation to a United Nations' programme on AIDS prevention. Mark delivered a powerful speech on the bold efforts to prevent and eradicate the disease in Zowambia. He had concluded his speech by advocating that out of the ABC options of preventing AIDS, he would want the world to stay in the middle of the road by sticking to option B; faithfulness to one's partner, as the best and practical option. Mark remembered that when journalists asked him why he believed the A and C options were not as effective, he had told them that abstinence could only be enforced on the under-aged and condom could fail if there was strong tornado before the rain. He remembered that there was a loud ovation when he compared low-quality condom to structurally defective umbrella or raincoats which would not and cannot stop rain from falling on the user.

Mark frowned and hissed as he remembered the irony of his speech when a few hours later, the supposedly HIV-free white lady invited to entertain him would not want a barrier to hinder the contacts between the long and robust black driller and the deep, luscious labyrinth for the ultimate search. Those thrilling eruption therein must have given birth to the present condition of his wife. Mark recalled sadly and hissed again.

'The President is lost in thought.' Labake observed as she heard the President hissing, the second time within a minute.

Mark had completely forgotten she was on seat. 'I am sorry, Labake. I become moody at every thought of this HIV thing.'

'I have told you that a person may test positive without showing AIDS symptoms. It is only when the immunity to the viral infection of HIV positive individual is broken down that the virus becomes deadly.'

'How will Maggy feel? How can I look at her directly in the eyes?' Mark lamented.

'Why are you sure you are the cause? The infection can come through other means. Injection, using infected sharp objects, transfusion and so on.'

'I was unfaithful to her, a few times, since the last time I tested negative.' Mark paused, and studied her face. He could see pity and affection for him in them. He continued. 'If you have not been highly disciplined, you would have been a victim of my lust.'

Labake considered what to say to remove the obvious guilty feeling of the President. 'But you told me you always go on condom unless it is Maggy.'

'Yes. That's true, but I remember an exception.' Mark closed his eyes briefly and opened them again. 'The woman I met in Washington, during the United Nations-sponsored seminar on AIDS, made me broke the rule. It was a naked encounter at her request and pleading.'

'And at the height of desire or passion, the B option was discarded by its number one proponent, and neither was the A option nor the wisdom and safety in the C option considered.'

Mark almost laughed at the way Labake configured his action. He saw the affection in her reprimand and accepted her annoyance with a smile.

'If you had been there for me when I needed company, I wouldn't be in this mess.'

'Don't blame me, Mr President. You could always travel with the First Lady but you still prefer to behave like any other man. You are not an ordinary citizen. You are the President of Zowambia. Your enemies are watching. There is no way it would not filter to them if I warm your bed during our frequent trips.' Labake moved from her seat and stood close to the President.

'Tongues have been wagging already.' Mark made her realised.

'But there is no witness or evidence to give credence to straying tongues.'

'A scandal involving you and me would have been better managed than what could come from the HIV scandal.'

'That's true.' Labake agreed. 'But there won't be any scandal. All we need to do is to block out Maggy of her condition. She needs not to know yet. You will need the cooperation of your friend, Doctor Bibilari.'

'He will do whatever I asked him to do.' The President assured her. 'Already, he is doing everything possible to make sure nobody besides the three of us knew about Maggy's case. I had to put him into confidence that I don't hide anything from you before he could forgive me for telling you the truth.'

'I noticed his occasional suspicious glances at me these two past dayss.' Labake reflected. 'I think it is time you stopped all sexual escapades if you want a second term. We would be lucky to pull through this without blemish.'

'Assure me of your readiness if the outcome of my test is negative. Then I will do away with any arranged entertainment on official outing.' The President said to her in a husky voice.

'If you test positive . . . ?'

'I will not touch you.' Mark was quick and convincing in his response. It will be Mark and Maggy forever. The real B option, until one of us completely submits to the ultimate result of the virus infection.'

'You are a wonderful boss.' Labake said, closing the gap between them.

'I would have loved to be a wonderful lover but for . . . '

Labake did not allow him to complete the sentence before their lips met. Lightly at first, then there was a passionate lipial search that activated the tongues, thus opening transmission lines to the entire body. They held, longitudinally poled, for a minute, before they separated. 'There is no HIV en-route kissing.' She said, rolled her tongue between her sensuous lips and touched his with a well-manicured forefinger.

'When I get back to Zowambia, I will arrange for another HIV test.' Mark said again after a little silence between them.

'Why?' Labake was surprised.

'I want to make love to you. It is what I've wanted so much but not as a HIV positive man.'

'You don't have to ruin your political career through such test.' Labake tried to dissuade him. 'There is the possibility of leakage of the result if it turns out you are infected.'

'Bibilari will handle it.'

'He will employ others to do it.'

The President considered this and smiled. 'It is a risk worth taking for your companionship, Labake. I know how to go about it discretely.' Mark smiled as he realised that he was ready to take the risk.

'I want you to be sure of what you intend to do. As for me, when I am ready for you, the virus scare will not be the determinant. I will want my President, our President to stop the drifting. Whatever the outcome of the test, I promise to give Mark a close mark henceforth. Only Maggy and I will receive generous donations from you, if you, really, are a donor. No more special entertainment henceforth, Mr. President.' She was determined to help Mark through this difficult time, even to the detriment of her own health.

'Your wish is my command, madam.' Mark smiled, still savouring the taste of their kiss. 'But it will be crazy if you zipped down for me if I am HIV-positive.'

Labake tried to change the subject. She thought it was time to let the President have a brief of the news. Economic news, first. The zowab depreciating against the dollar as the foreign oil workers in Zowambia stayed away from work on security grounds. Next, the political news: Many party faithful are defecting to the opposition party because the President wants a second term. The reason for the defection was their belief that the ZNP would lose the election because of the tight fiscal and economic policies of Okuta's administration.

Next, the social news: The President is reported holidaying in London in order to be close to his wife recuperating from a road accident between Longbridge and Seaview.

The phone rang and Labake stopped to allow the President to receive it.

'Who is this?' Mark didn't like the interruption.

'IB, Mr. President.' Idoh identified himself. He was using a public phone. 'I just had a chat with the director of Embassy Hospital. The preliminary findings during the autopsy on Ivy suggested cardiac arrest. She was neither raped nor murdered.' He lay emphasis on the last sentence to let the President know he was not a suspect.

'That's comfortable, IB, thanks.' Mark dropped the phone and gave Labake the story.

'I am sure Doctor Bibilari would prefer whoever knew about the HIV-status of Maggy dead, himself inclusive.' Labake summed up after listening to Mark expressing his fear of Idoh's involvement in the matter. When the President did not respond, she added, 'You need to watch him closely.'

'Why?'

'He wouldn't mind if the First Lady dies so that the scandal could be completely buried.' Labake said, in all innocence.

'That's going too far. Idoh is fond of Maggy.' Mark objected.

'Didn't you also at times think he was behaving funny? I saw something in him. Obsession or fear, I am not sure. Heed my advice, Mr. President. Monitor your friend. He is not being closely monitored.'

Mark nodded in agreement in order to stop the trend of the discussion. He did not buy the idea but pretended to do so. Idoh had always been his enthusiastic self in anything he believed in, the second term is one of such things.

XXXXX

At noon the next day, the President and his entourage were met on arrival from London, by his deputy, Ahmed Mando. Journalists were there in their tens. They welcome him with questions on the health of the first lady.

'Was it true that the doctor in charge of our First Lady died in her sleep on Tuesday?' It was *Daily News* correspondent that threw the first salvo.

The President just smiled and told the journalist to talk to the press officer.

'Is that so, Madam?' The journalist put her microphone close to Labake's mouth.

'Yes. She was suspected to have died of cardiac arrest in her bathroom.'

'The first doctor who handled the case here, Dr Fred Agbamuche died, too. Are you aware of this?' another correspondent asked.

'Yes.' Labake Pedro smiled. 'He died in one of those acts of reckless driving on the express bridge.'

'Did the President, at any time, since, suspect foul play?' a third newspaperman asked.

'Why should he . . . ?' Labake frowned. 'Not, at all. The incidents became big news because the first lady was their patient.

'Is it true that the President's campaign for ZNP nomination ticket for a second term flags off at Golas tomorrow?' *The Sun Times* reporter wanted to confirm the speculative news in some rival newspaper.

Labake smiled as she responded. 'You are right about the date. There is going to be a rally for Mark Okuta's second coming. Tomorrow is the flag off date. It is going to take place in Gadas, not Golas. Charity, they say, begins at home.

Mark has decided to flag off his campaign from his birthplace and follow up with rallies in Santa-bayel and Santa-osha that same day.' With that said, Mrs. Labake Pedro entered her own vehicle, next to the President's in the convoy that took them to the Seaview Fortress.

The President saw the remnants of the vehicle that killed Doctor Fred and two others as they drove through the express bridge. He wondered why the police and the National Guard had failed to clear the mess in order to avoid another catastrophe. Somebody would be held responsible for the lapses, he promised himself. He called the attention of his Protocol Officer in the third vehicle to note the ugly trap and make sure it is not there before nightfall.

xxxxx

A week after the political rally at Mark's hometown, Gadas, Maggy came back from London. She had completely recovered from the accident. The suture was fast healing up and the stitches would be removed soon. She entered her office in the Seaview Fortress and the picture of her husband confronted her on the television. It was health news time on the national television, ZTN, and she frowned as Mark hugged and shook hands with AIDS patients.

Idoh saw her look. 'Is there anything wrong?' he asked her.

'Look,' she pointed to the telly, 'he is hugging and shaking hands with AIDS patients.'

'What's wrong with that?' Idoh was surprised that the First Lady who had on many occasions condemned the stigmatisation of AIDS victims could have such reaction.

'Many things had gone wrong doctor, many things.' Maggy said seriously, turning to Idoh and away from the television that was repeating her husband address to the attentive and elated victims of AIDS. 'Mark shouldn't allow our political statements on the dreaded disease override his reasoning. He had started hugging AIDS victims, he might get carried away one of these days and kiss victims publicly.

'What's wrong if he does?' Idoh could not believe he heard Maggy well. She had been pictured in the past where she was helping a child victim to put on her dress.

'That would be the last day he would kiss me.' Maggy's voice was dead serious.

Mark had just entered to welcome his wife. He had the last part of her sentence. 'What are you talking about?'

'It is women's usual worries, Mr. President.' Idoh quickly answered. He didn't want the President to know how she felt about HIV-positive persons. He thought the President will be devastated because of her disposition.

'You said it's women talk?' Maggy snapped. 'Don't deceive your friend, doctor. Tell him how I feel about HIV-positive people. I hate people going about dipping their spoon in every pot of porridge available.'

'It is not only through sex that one becomes infected with HIV.' Mark got into the picture.

'But in most cases, it is sexually transmitted. In all cases I had talked to, it is the one-minute pleasure that led to their everlasting sorrow.' Maggy talked rapidly.

At that point, Mark was admonishing the deadly virus victims on the television not to lose hope as his administration would do everything possible to make life comfortable for them and should avoid being socially ostracized which could lead to serious depression.

'Sex is not always the cause, Maggy.' Mark tried to explain. 'Careless blood transfusion, genetic fusion, injection, intravenous applications are some of the causes.'

'Just don't bring HIV to this family because of political gains you expect in return of your political showmanship.'

'So you won't kiss me if I test positive?' Mark wanted to confirm her earlier statement he overheard.

Maggy's smile was sardonic. She got up and came close to her husband. 'Who will want to dine with the devil? Only a fool. My children are young and I am expecting the big one.' She touched her belly. 'If you test positive, Mr. President, I will only remain First Lady or Mrs. Okuta if we don't have to do anything together than public appearance.' She stated as a matter-of-fact, and with a tone of finality.

Mark smiled but Idoh felt uncomfortable. 'We could still kiss even though we abstain from sex until . . . '

'I am waiting,' Maggy cut in as Mark left the sentence hanging. 'There is no cure for AIDS. I don't believe there will ever be. I won't want to live with an AIDS victim even if he is President of America.'

'But you will, if he is your darling, Mark Okuta, the President of Zowambia.'

Maggy looked at her husband thoughtfully, then suspiciously. 'Are you positive? Is that what you are trying to tell me?' She started drawing back, almost running away from his reach. She would have entered the wall without being conscious of what she was doing. She hated to be near an HIV victim again. No more politics of HIV-AIDS. She had told herself after the last time she had her test which confirmed her negative status.

'The President is trying to let you know more about HIV and AIDS.' Idoh saw the confusion on Mark and understood the hurt in his eyes.

Mark had kissed Maggy several times after the confirmation of her positive status. Though he was feeling guilty that he might be the cause, he felt betrayed and disappointed at his wife's reaction to his question.

'Perhaps I should go for a test in order for me to have your full attention.' The President told her sarcastically what he had actually done the previous day.

'I won't mind if we all do so, darling.' Maggy smiled for the first time. 'Maybe Ivy would have done mine in London.'

'Welcome home, my lady.' The President said, he felt bitter at his wife's behaviour. Yet, he still brought out a bunch of rose flower he was hiding into view. 'This is for you darling,' he said with a pretentious smile. 'At least I should take a kiss for this unless you are still virus scared.' With that, the President held Maggy closer and they kissed, like a newly wedded.

The doctor wondered how deep the love Mark had for his wife was. He wondered still at his inner strength to keep the Maggy's condition unknown to her at that point when she had bluntly told Mark she would not have anything to do with him if he tested positive. It was an unconditional love exhibited by Mark, and Idoh admired him for it.

xxxxx

The lab technician of the diagnostic centre that handled the blood test of Mark Okuta and Labake Pedro came in with the result to the latter. The President was at his wife's office, a distance of five hundred metres away.

'Both couples are free to marry.' The lab man told Labake. 'They both tested negative to HIV.' He held the result for her to see.

Mrs. Labake's heart skipped some beats. She was temporarily dumbfounded. She was sure her blood would test negative because she had had total sexual abstinence since the last time she tested negative. But the President's blood result marvelled her. What happened? Where did the First Lady get contacted? Was she having an affair outside wedlock? Who would want to play around with the President's wife? Who is the President's wife dating? Could it be through those other sources, that no AIDS victims had openly declared, that led to their problem? The news is going to be both interesting and devastating to the President. He loved his wife and he would feel betrayed. She didn't know how Mark would handle this but she knew he would handle it in a manner that the end result would not affect his future political plans.

When Labake did not respond, the lab-technician decided to tell her the problem the new couple might encounter if they got married. 'Madam, the lady would need some hormone treatment. Her level of progesterone and other related sex hormones need to be boosted in order for pregnancy not to be delayed.' The lab man and the doctor had been misled that the blood samples belonged to Labake's cousin and her boyfriend, a much younger couple.

'That would be arranged when they get to London. There won't be any problem.' She spread her hand to take the paper from him. 'How soon can I have the comprehensive report of this?'

'By noon tomorrow, Madam.'

'Thank you.' As Labake got up from her seat, the lab man knew the meeting was over. He was relishing the opportunity he had to work for somebody in the Seaview Fortress. Had he known he was handling the President's blood, the whole world would have been told of this most important job.

An hour later, Mrs. Labake Pedro was in the company of her boss to welcome the new envoy from Italy. After the meeting, Labake drew the President to a corner and told him the result of their blood test. As expected, there was a sparkle of delight, followed immediately by a look of concern in President

Mark Okuta. He tried hard to control his emotion in the public.

'Thank you, Labake.' He finally beamed a smile as they both walked out of the reception room to the next appointment. Chiefs from Gadas and other villages in his home local government had come for a solidarity visit. Their gong and traditional instruments made a local melody composed for their most illustrious son, Mark Okuta.

xxxxx

'You came to welcome me in the office.' Maggy turned on the bed to face her husband. She allowed a sensuous smile to play on her lips. 'Won't you welcome me to the house?' She kissed him lightly on the lip while her movement allowed her bare body to rub on his hairy chest.

'Welcome darling.' He responded and returned her kiss.

She smiled, drawing a line with her finger from his forehead to his navel. 'Is that all you want after many days of hunger?'

He looked at her seductive posture again and kissed her eager lips. Then, her breasts found their way in turn to his warm mouth.

'I am back, Mark.' She said as his tongue triggered some erotic motion in her.

'Welcome home, my love.' Mark managed to say, and tactically moved away from under her.

She waited expectantly for his next move. When it wouldn't come, she asked, 'Won't you visit the shrine?'

'The shrine needs cleaning first.' Mark said in a serious undertone.

'I don't understand you, Mark. Or you have been messing around.'

'Stop that Maggy!' Mark snapped. 'You have to flush out that baby. It is going to be a girl. I don't think I can have a boy.' He concealed the real reason why the baby must not be allowed to develop.

Maggy felt cold. 'I thought you hate abortion, Mr. President.'

'I do.'

'You don't, Sir.' Maggy was annoyed. 'If you do, you won't ask me to abort my baby.'

'It is our baby, Maggy.' The President reminded her.

'Yes, our unborn baby.' Maggy took the correction. She believed that with her cooperation, Doctor Bibilari had been able to get a sample of Mark's sperm on three different occasions. She understood that this would be treated outside the body and the culture introduced to her womb, scientifically. This was successful after a third trial.

'I am not a killer. But nowadays every child coming into the world must have the chance of survival. You have just had a blood transfusion. You may not have a right environment inside you for the baby now.' Mark tried to convince her.

'Okay. I'll see doctor Bibilari tomorrow.'

'That's my wife.'

'Seeing the Doctor tomorrow doesn't prevent us from making love today, tonight. Now!'

'Let's wait until the doctor is sure or not sure the baby will be okay. Besides, it may be too early in your trimester to allow in the chief priest.' Mark kissed her and turned away from her on the bed.

She had lovemaking on her mind all day, and she found it difficult to put her mind off the matrimonial right that her husband denied her on the excuse of the unborn baby. It took her some time after, before she could sleep.

XXXXX

President Mark Okuta left the official residence inside the Seaview Fortress very early the following morning. He drove himself across the gardens until he got to the security guards at the Eastern gate. Apparently, the guards did not recognise it was the President until one of them peeped in.

'It is the Excellency!' He shouted and others became alert and stood up involuntarily to take a salute. 'This is not right, Sir. We can't allow you out of the Fortress without escorts.'

Mark smiled. 'I don't need one. No protocols. I am in a hurry to see the family doctor at Zango Kataf Avenue. I am not going beyond the Fortress.' He smiled again.

'You will be followed, Sir.' Without waiting for approval, the guards signalled two security vehicles' Mark didn't need them but he knew the men were doing their job. He wondered if he would ever be allowed to be alone with anybody, apart from his wife. He was driving in the middle of the two security vehicles at a speed determined by the forerunner. He wondered if the driver knew his destination. When the vehicle slowed down on approaching Idoh's apartment, Mark realised they knew the terrain more than himself.

Idoh was at the door to receive him. 'What are you doing here, Mark?' The visit was unusual.

Mark motioned him to move inside the house before he spoke. 'I tested negative.'

'That can't be true.' Idoh responded to the news. Then he realised he had been unfair to Mark in his comment. 'Rather, I wanted to say where did Maggy catch the bug?'

'That's why I am here, IB.'

'Who conducted your test?' Idoh felt left out.

'Labake did it discretely at Longbridge Diagnostic Center in Downtown. It was meant for a couple about to wed.' Mark revealed.

'Who took the samples?'

'It was taken by one of the-nurses known very well to Labake. She works at National Hospital.'

'That's it.' Idoh snapped. 'The Vice President called me after our meeting in your wife's office yesterday to ask if everything is okay with the First Lady. He wanted to know if anything is wrong with her blood.' Idoh added with emphasis on the word blood. 'I told the VP that the transfused blood integrated perfectly with hers.'

'Was he convinced?' Mark asked

'He wasn't.' Idoh paused. 'Ahmed said he was wondering why some blood samples were taken for test again by the press officer and personal assistant to the President.'

'Why can't he call me and ask?' Mark suspected ill motive in his deputy's inquisitiveness.

'He said he wondered why I wasn't involved.'

The President dismissed the whole thing with a wave of the hand. 'Ahmed thought the two samples belonged to Maggy and I. Luckily, the two samples tested negative. That would put paid to speculations. If it were to be the other way round, it would have been like washing our dirty linen in the public.' Mark said satisfactorily.

'It would have been bye to the second term.' Idoh put it more directly.

Mark looked at his wristwatch. He had an appointment with Labake in a quarter of an hour. 'I think it is your responsibility to let Maggy know her status.'

'We could keep her ignorant until after the election.'

'How do I avoid her without suspicion? Besides, how did she come about HIV? At least she doesn't believe it could be contacted through any other means. She must have been sleeping around. Get the truth out of her. I had her booking appointment with you for today. I'll call you at noon.' The President was out before Idoh could open his mouth.

Idoh was lost in thought. The First Lady had been very decent since he knew her. It was only the issue of absence of male child that had ever made her talk to him about their sexual relationship. She had said the President had been fantastic besides the fact that he could not give her a son. It was a genetical problem. Idoh remembered he started her treatment. He had been very careful and he had ensured that the culture used would provide the desired result. Maggy must have gone out of the confines of her treatment to meet an infected man in her drive for a baby boy, he thought.

A few minutes after the President's private visit Idoh was crossing the Zakibiam Valley to the main areas of Seaview Fortress. He arrived at Fortress Clinic situated on Odi Crescent early enough, to prepare for the arrival of Maggy.

xxxxx

Labake was waiting for the President at 8am. The offices will not be filled up with activities until 9am. She had an idea of the intention of the President early call to her office. She was prepared for him. She had told the security officer at the entrance not to allow anybody into the office until she finished the speech writing for the President. He should let her assistants know that the President didn't want any distraction, even from the VP or Maggy.

Mark opened her door quietly and entered. He turned to lock at the door.

'Don't worry, Mr. President, the door is automatically secured. Besides, we are not staying here. We'll use the back entrance to reach my apartment. My children have all gone back to school, you know.' Labake smiled as she stood up to meet him, holding a remote control for the door. They took the back exit to her apartment adjoining the office.

'You read my mind.' Mark said, surveying the room he was entering for the first time.

'There are no cameras, no bugs.' She smiled again. 'We are alone.'

'How do you know that's what I want?' Mark was surprised at her quickness.

'Your body language, Mr. President. I am prepared for the celebration. Besides I don't want you to make wrong moves, as the First Lady is unavailable, at this crucial moment.'

'It is going to be all the way. You know.'

'Don't command me, Mark.' She put a little bite in her sensuous voice. 'I know you are in a killer mood. All I demand of you is to kill me slowly and lovingly.' She smiled as she expertly removed her flowing gown to expose her smooth skin underneath.

Mark saw her fullness. The figure of a forty-five year old that looked like twenty-five, thrilled him. He removed his own outfit in seconds. 'I can't believe we'll celebrate it here, Labake.'

'Stop talking and get the gun loaded to discharge its bullet.' Labake walked into his open hands. A few minutes after sharing a long preparatory kiss, the two bodies melt into one . . .

'I love you, Labake.' He said as they disengaged, several minutes later.

'No, Mark.' She shook her head. 'You enjoyed our lovemaking. I had a fantastic voyage too.' She reflected on their union; the steady ascent to the mountain top, the cloud nine at the peak and the slow dive into the valley of temporary death, and the instantaneous resurrection. It is not love, she was convinced. It was bodily fulfillment, the animal in man. She remained calm and a kind of guilty feeling enveloped her. It was her first physical union with a man in five years. Funny enough she knew she was coming in to Mark's life for real. 'You are lost in thought, Labake.'

'You are right. I am reviewing the act. I realized that no matter how strong you are as a woman, one still needs a man.' She smiled.

'That's what Maggy told me yesterday after I refused to have fun.'

'It is a fact.' She was silent for a while. 'I am suggesting that you find out how and where she got infected.'

'I'll put a bug on her when going to the clinic.'

'Why?'

'She might tell the doctor what she won't tell me. Is her status not bothering you?'

'It surely does, Mr. President.'

'Then let's get to the root of how she contacted it. It doesn't matter anymore if anybody knows. It is definitely not from me. I will leave that to you and Suara to handle'

Once more, they explored the route they had travelled half an hour earlier. It was a slower but steadier journey and this time, it took them a longer period to reach their destination.

At the strike of 9a.m., the President was seen coming out of Labake's office with a file. He veered from his own office to the direction of Maggy's.

xxxxx

First Lady Maggy Okuta was looking good in her Senegalese attire as she stepped out of her office and walked smartly to the parking lot where her driver was already running the engine. She discovered another policewoman had replaced the injured Hauwa. She grimaced at the thought of Hauwa becoming disabled as a result of the injuries sin the Longbridge accident. She had other things to think about now, more pressing questions that needed answer. Only Doctor Bibilari could help to put her mind at rest.

She had been told by her husband to find out from the family doctor if the pregnancy was reasonable. He said something about the health of the baby she could not understand. He was so cold to her on the bed the previous night but he came to her office, moment ago, looking healthy, relaxed and enthusiastically warm. He had advised her to tell their family doctor all she would want to know about the unborn baby. The thought that she might be the one that was not healthy came to her and she shivered as she was entering into the backseat of the car.

During his brief stop over in her office earlier, Vice President Mando had revealed to her that Doctor Fred died on his way to London carrying her blood sample. The VP had expressed his happiness over her health and the fact that everything was perfect with the blood transfused to her system. She was determined to ask questions when she got to the Fortress Clinic.

When they got to the clinic, she did not wait for the police officer to open the car door. She alighted from the car quickly and walk-ran into the clinic where Idoh was waiting.

'Good morning, madam.' Doctor Idoh greeted.

'Good morning, doctor.' She responded.

Idoh ushered her into the private room reserved for the first family. Her new police aide followed, took out the tiny powerful recorder she had, set it on and dropped it inside the First Lady's handbag. Inside the room, Maggy turned to the aide, 'Put my bag on the table, Sergeant, and go outside.'

She felt reluctant but obeyed and withdrew from the room as Maggy took her seat opposite the doctor's. Her handbag sat on the table, between them. Sergeant Lisa Pedro, a relation of Labake, switched on the receiver and listened to the exchanges between Maggy and Idoh through an earpiece.

'Well, Maggy.' Idoh started familiarly, 'You are one hour early.'

'I can't wait, doctor. I had things troubling my mind.'

'Let me carry the burden.' Idoh gave his trademark response.

Maggy told him the discussion he had with Mark the previous night and concluded her narration in tears. 'Mark refused to make love to me. It had never happened since we got married.' She was in tears, and Lisa listening outside, felt pity for her.

'Don't let that bother you. He is only being considerate for your health and the baby's.' Idoh knew he wasn't telling her the true reason for Mark's behaviour.

Maggy shook her head. 'It could not be for the baby he has no interest in having.'

'What do you think was his reason, then?' Idoh asked, looking at her intensely.

'Tell me, doctor.' Maggy leant forward towards Idoh and kept her voice low. 'Is Mark in any trouble? Is he having the disease?'

'What disease are you talking about?' Idoh was surprised the first lady is suspecting her husband.

'AIDS.' Maggy put across casually. 'I know he was a randy dog in those days but I knew he was using condom with his mistresses for my sake, then.'

'The President is decent.' Idoh tried to defend his friend.

'You'll defend him. He's your friend and president. Your loyalty is more to him. What is his problem?'

'Mark has no problem, no HIV infection.'

'That was two years and a half ago, doctor. Mark must have slept with a dozen women since then. Who knows?' Maggy put her thought and conviction in words.

'It is not fair on your husband.' Idoh stated how he felt, considering what he knew of their problem. 'What if your husband thought you are having an affair too?'

'That would be ridiculous. Where, when and how? You know it is not possible. If any other person had had access to his property since we've got married, it is you, doctor.'

'I touched you on professional basis, madam.'

'Yes, during examination, child bearing and the latest IVF treatments.' Maggy further explained.

'I agreed.' Idoh said. 'That's not messing around. What I mean is real affair with other men?'

'I will never cheat on Mark. So far, he had been capable of making me happy. You know what I mean, doctor.'

Idoh considered how to tell her that she was the problem but his professional confidence failed him as that thought crossed his mind again. He opted to delay the revelation until he knew his own status, too. 'I will have to take your blood sample for lab test, madam. This is necessary to ascertain your status and that of the child.' As an afterthought he added, 'It is the new approach to Medicare for all pregnant women.'

'I am not interested.' Maggy stood up in protest, and sat down again. 'The last two occasions when my blood sample was taken, the doctors died miraculously. I won't allow it to happen to you. I am beginning to think that there is an instant poison in my blood that kills. Don't give me a bad name, doctor.'

'We know why those doctors died, Maggy. We sacrificed them to protect you, to prevent a political and social scandal.'

Idoh admitted he had the knowledge of the deaths of Fred and Ivy.

'Come again, doctor? You committed murder because of me? Mark killed to keep scandalous news?'

'No, Maggy. Mark is not a murderer. He didn't know about the killings. He won't approve such but I helped him, as a friend and as the family doctor.'

'But why, why, why did you kill the woman you dated? I suspected all along that you had a hand in her death.'

'She did a test on you to confirm your HIV-status, Maggy.'

'I am HIV . . .' Maggy could not complete the sentence.

'Positive.' Idoh rushed to hold her and calmed her down.

She started to sob. After about two minutes she was completely calm 'Mark would not kill because of scandal. He would have voluntarily stepped down from seeking a second term. I know my Mark.'

'But he wanted the condition hidden from you at all cost. Because I knew that Doctor Ivy Douglas will spill the bean, I had to take care of her, and Fred knew too much and was blown out earlier. He was loyal to the VP. I had to arrange the trailer that rammed into the Limo.'

'Did Mark know this?'

'He didn't know. The saint won't approve it. It was my scheme. Mark must go for a second term.'

Maggy Okuta stood up and paced the small room, looked at herself in the mirror and shook her head. 'How do I face Mark now?'

'You don't have to worry. He had been coping with the news. He had done everything possible to make you feel wanted, even when he found out that he is HIV-negative.'

'Where did I contact this, then, if not from him?' 'That's the big question, Maggy. Once again: do you have an affair with any other man besides the President?'

'Not since I got married to him?

'Let's narrow it to the last two years since you last took the test together during the public awareness campaign you sponsored.' Idoh probed further.

'I didn't have sex with any other man, doctor.' She paused. 'The only other man I had contact with is you. I mean the treatment you gave me. Those professional visits inside my down below.'

The doctor was silent, thinking. Maggy continued. 'But you told me it was my husband's sperm you mixed with some hormones to give the right culture for our desired result.'

Idoh Bibilari was scared as Maggy reminded him of the treatment she had approved for herself. Idoh had told Maggy that he would talk Mark into donating in-vitro for the culture to be prepared before introducing it to Maggy.

Idoh never consulted Mark, who he knew had less than ten percent chance of producing sperm with male chromosome. He had gone ahead to use his own sperm on three different occasions within a year. The third attempt had been successful. Idoh was afraid that he might be the one that transmitted HIV to the first lady. He wasn't sure of his HIV-status. He had never taken the test.

'I am not sure there was no foul play, Maggy. Unless you contacted HIV through other means, other than sex.'

That's impossible. I had been very careful.' She paused. 'Despite the result of Mark's blood test, I'll still hold him responsible for my condition because we still had fun regularly despite the treatment. And you doctor, as a friend of Mark, I trusted your decision. Who knows what you connived and introduced into my womb?' She was silent for while, and then smiled ruefully. 'I know now. It is AIDS from God-knows-where or from Mark.'

Doctor Idoh Bibilari was sweating inside the air-conditioned room. The only chance he had to avoid the scandal was to discourage her from talking to her husband further on the issue. The realisation that he was the person who infected Maggy frightened him. Besides, he had committed a professional misconduct that could not be pardoned. He would be ruined if the facts were known. 'Let me talk to Mark on this before you do.' Idoh managed to say.

'I am calling him right now, doctor.' She brought out her phone and started to dial.

Idoh was afraid and desperate. He quickly crossed to the other side of the table and took the phone from her. 'I can't allow you to call him, Your Excellency.' He resulted to official protocol.

'Why?' The First Lady was surprised at how jumpy Idoh had become.

'The President didn't know about the treatment you had.'

'What!' Maggy frowned and looked enquiringly. 'But the sperm culture you introduced into . . . . '

'They were not his.' Idoh said, passively. He was on his knees in front of Maggy.

Maggy's heart was beating fast, in anger. 'Who, whose thing did you put inside me?' She closed her eyes in disgust, and shame.

Idoh could not answer. 'I am sorry, Your Excellency.'

'Quit that nonsense. I am not excellent. I am filthy and unworthy of honour.' She was heaving and the movement of her breasts reflected the fast rate of her heartbeats. 'Whose sperm or rather, whose HIV-baby is inside my womb?'

Idoh could not look up to meet her eyes. 'Mine.' He said feebly.

'Yours?' she chuckled in anger. 'You indirectly made love to me. Jesus Christ! And all the while I opened up submissively thinking that Mark was a loving husband to have gone the extra mile to make me happy. You led me into believing your lies. Now I am a HIV woman. I'll call Mark.'

'You can't do so.' Idoh stood up and went swiftly to the cabinet containing drugs. 'We must get rid of the pregnancy, then start treatment of the HIV. He took a syringe, brought out a well-concealed bottle of cyanide, inserted the needle and started to draw the content into the syringe.

'Doctor.' Maggie called his attention. I will not take any treatment from you until I talk to my husband.' She started to dial the President's hotline.

Idoh quickly dropped the syringe, put his hand in his overcoat and drew out a pistol. Maggy saw the pistol. 'What's that for?'

'If you don't put that phone down Maggy, I'll blow your head.' Idoh said without emotion.

Lisa was becoming impatient outside. The gadget on her could not pick the exchanges inside but the pitch of the muddled noise made her felt uneasy. She used the walkie-talkie to alert Labake. She restrained herself from bursting into the party for two, inside. Suddenly the receiver in her ear came alive and she listened.

'Now I believe you are a killer.' Maggy was the first she picked.

'I am not denying that.' Idoh's voice was threatening.

'Killing me does not take away your infection, Doctor.'

'It will take away my shame. Nobody will ever know what happened. You killed yourself, suicide. You could not bear to face Mark with your shame. Infidelity, HIV. He would give you a befitting burial. Nobody would know the whole story. Only IB will know what happened.'

'Don't kill me. The President can still forgive you.'

'This is beyond pardon. Put down the phone, Maggy.' He pointed the gun at her forehead as the phone rang at the other end. Idoh took the phone from her at gunpoint. He cocked the gun and she closed her eyes.

'Maggy, I hope you are alright.' Mark said at the other end.

'This is IB, Mark. Maggy could not stand the news.' He was moving away from Maggy as he spoke and aimed his gun at her forehead. 'She had just shot herself, Your Excellency.' As he pulled the trigger, the policewoman forced the door opened and fired at Idoh. Her intervention was seconds too late as two bullets had found their way into the First Lady's chest. The impact of the bullets forced her from standing position to her chair.

Meanwhile, Idoh's pistol dropped from his hand at the impact of Lisa's shot that hit him on the right shoulder. The policewoman rushed to the First Lady who was already gasping. In her confusion she hurried back to the door. As she opened it, she saw President Mark and Labake coming towards her direction.

Mark was still holding the phone to his ear. He took in the situation as he entered. 'I hope you are not hurt.' He said to his wife as he entered and saw the almost lifeless Maggy gaping at the void in sitting position. He bent down to feel her breath, and noticed the blood spot on her chest. 'Jesus Christ!' he exclaimed as he carried her almost lifeless body to the open space on the carpeted floor. Labake hurried back to the entrance to for help and Lisa went after Idoh's gun reaching it before the owner. With both guns pointed at him, Idoh dragged his legs painfully towards the drug cabinet. The doctor appeared oblivious of Lisa's close mark as he took a small bottle and drank the content.

'Stop!' Lisa commanded. 'You still have the gut to go for a drink.'

The President looked up from his dying wife and saw the bottle dropped by Idoh rolling towards his direction and stopped at the edge of the carpet. The President looked at the doctor and picked the bottle. Poison. He looked from the bottle to the doctor and then Lisa. 'What's going on?' he shouted at Idoh.

'Goodnight, Mark.' Idoh managed to say with a sardonic smile.

'Please, speak to me.' Mark pleaded and came closer to the doctor.

Idoh opened his mouth in pain. The gunshots had weakened him and the poison was having a damaging effect on his vital organs. 'You will never know, Mark.' He smiled again, and slumped in the process of speaking further.

The appearance of Labake with the ambulance men did not allow Mark to give his medical aide and friend a helping hand. Mark watched the ambulance doctor searching frantically for life in Maggy. He shook his head sadly as he was led away from the scene by his Chief Security Officer.

xxxxx

The funeral ceremony for Maggy was brief. Lying in state took place in the open soccer stadium in Gadas. A few enemies, political associates and opponents of Mark playing with their faces, we'll-miss-you-Maggy, we-love-you-but—God-loves-you-more, but they were unanimous in their silent condemnation of the probable cause of the death. The official silence on the autopsy report fueled the suspicion that the truth had not been told by the presidency.

The funeral procession to the burial ground was limited to family members, clergy men, selected political associates and foreign envoys. Maggy's family members were barred from the final phase of the ceremony. They clamoured that Golas should have the remains of the First Lady. She was a Golan and custom demanded she must be committed to mother earth in Golas. President Mark Okuta had vetoed the decision to bury his wife where and how he wanted.

As the body was being lowered to the grave, the supporters of custom and Golans protested a hundred metres away from the country home of Mark, where the burial was taking place.

Labake Pedro was ambushed by the press correspondents as the crowd thinned out after the burial. They wanted more information on the death that was described as one death too many. Five days had gone by, and all they were fed with were mere rumours and unofficial comments:

-The First Lady did not recover her good health after the crash at Longbridge.

-Maggy was shot by her family doctor in order to cover their illicit affair.

-Maggy committed suicide in reaction to her HIV status.

-Is the President HIV positive too?

-First Lady murdered few hours after her police aide was changed.

—Who is Lisa Pedro?

Now that the burial was over, the news hunters thought that Mark or any spokesperson from the presidency should speak to them.

'Tell us the cause of death.' This was the common denominator of the journalists' questions.

Labake, dressed in a black and white dress for the mourning mood in the presidency, almost lost her cool as the men blocked her way. She quickly gained control of her irritation as she noticed that television cameras were on her too. 'First Lady Maggy Okuta died from the trigger pulled by Dr. Bibilari. Lisa Pedro, the police officer seconded to the First Lady was fractions of a second late at preventing the situation.'

They were not satisfied. They knew what had happened and who were involved. They wanted to know why it happened. That was the expectation of Zowambians and the international communities.

'Doctor Bibilari will soon have enough energy to speak.' She gave a cynical smile. 'Until then we shall continue to feed on the rumours making the round.'

The police officer should know, they protested.

'She knew what happened but not the reason for it. She reacted to the situation she met on re-entering the room.' Labake paused. 'Ladies and gentlemen, let us wait a few more days for Doctor Bibilari to fill in the gaps. Until then, President Okuta will not speak on the action of his friend and family doctor. Let us hope that doctors in the national hospital will be successful in flushing out the poison in his blood completely.'

The newsmen grimaced as they dispersed. All they learnt was not enough for front page story for their various newspapers. Yes, murder had been officially confirmed. The reason for murder is the news which only Doctor Bibilari could provide.

The newsmen had a consensus that a big scandal had reared its head in ugliness in the presidency. They wondered why the easy-going state house physician should kill the First Lady.

The stories that appeared in the newspapers the following day gave a brief life history of Idoh. His academic exploits, his intelligence, his love for teaching, his success in practice, his long time friendship with President Okuta, and his unflinching loyalty to him. All the papers agreed on one point: unlike when the lure for wealth and fame made him abandon scholarship as the best anatomy lecturer in Zowambia, to a successful private practice, the movement to the present job in the presidency was out of the love for his good friend, Mark Okuta.

When the vice president read the newspapers the following day, he concluded that Idoh would do everything possible to conceal the truth if such would bring Mark, his friend to ridicule. He decided to visit him before anyone else did so. The matron in the National Hospital would do anything for him, if such is within her official capacity. She just had to be vigilant and alert to know almost immediately Idoh came to.

Ahmed dialled the number of the matron who answered promptly. 'I wonder if you have not touched the wrong buttons, Mr. V.P.' It was the voice of a forgotten mistress.

'I am sorry, Aisha. It is the pressure of the job.'

'I understand, Your Excellency,' she paused and added in a sarcastic tone, 'there must be pressure if we are as many as I know.'

'I am sorry.' The VP pleaded.

Matron Aisha became suspicious. 'Did I hear you say sorry a second time? I am sure there's more to this call than just to say hello.'

'Why?'

'You don't normally say sorry. It is not a word in your dictionary. It is this way if you need a favour.' She paused. 'I know you don't have time for me, Mr. VP, but tell me what you need.'

Vice President Mando was amused that his childhood lover would always be there for him despite the busy schedule that disallowed him from seeing her regularly as he promised when she lost her husband to another woman. Childlessness was the reason.

Ahmed arranged a meeting with her. He wouldn't want to discuss Idoh on the phone. He had some plan to overtake Mark in the campaign for the party's nomination ticket.

xxxxx

'Are you ready to talk on Idoh's case?' Labake asked the president as the last visitor left.

'What else do we discuss, Labake?' When Mark received no response, he stood up and brought out the cassette recorder. 'I have listened to the content several times.'

'I want to know what you have decided,' Labake knew that the president had made up his mind on what to do.

He came to her seat and patted her on the arm. 'If it was not for your smartness or instinct or both, this death would have been a mystery.' He turned around to face her. 'I would have believed Idoh. I would have wondered how long she had been cheating on me, and with whom. I would have hated her, or rather; I would have regretted falling in love with her. I wouldn't have been able to trust any woman again. I would have considered all her fidelity talk and my confessions and her pretences . . . '

Labake cut in. 'Thank God that you know the truth. The late First Lady was too passionate, too loving to go down a discredited woman. Thank God.'

'I should equally thank you for the tape and your choice of a smart police aide who knew what to do.'

'But Lisa failed.' Labake voiced out her opinion on the role she gave to her sister-in-law. 'The First Lady died.'

'It's not her fault.' Mark rose to her defense. 'She carried out her instruction to the letter. She planted the tape. Every other thing she did was by her own intuition.'

Labake nodded in agreement. 'I have told her to stick to her story. She opened the door and saw Idoh point his gun at Maggy . . . . '

'IB will corrfirm her story whenever he's fully recovered to speak.' Mark cut in.

'What's your decision on him?' Labake asked again.

Mark smiled. It was the first smile since the burial ended the previous day. 'It is Maggy, I blamed for this. Why should she want a baby boy at all cost and without my consent? I thought she was intelligent. Why should she believe that arrangement without my discussing it with her? It was stubbornness that killed her.'

Labake shook her head in disagreement. 'It wasn't stubbornness. It was love, and fear borne out of love.'

'That's your opinion, not mine.'

'President Mark is an African. Every African man, unless he is a catholic priest, wants a male child to carry on his name. Even eunuchs desire such. Your late wife was afraid that another woman might steal what belongs to her in your quest to have a male child.'

'But I constantly assured her.'

'And she constantly didn't believe you.' Labake's voice was serious. 'That's why she went ahead to do it. The hormonal boost deception by her trusted doctor and husband's friend.'

'I read disgust in her voice when Idoh confessed.'

'That's convincing enough for you about the fidelity of your darling wife.'

There was silence between them. The telephone rang, thus breaking into their thoughts. It was the Vice President on the hot line for Mark.

The news.

Doctor Idoh Bibilari was in a critical condition at the national hospital. Doctors said his condition was bad and hopeless. It was the mildest way of reporting a certainty. Death. Ahmed didn't want to tell the President the bad news on the phone. He considered it to be another devastating tragic moment for the presidency.

Before Idoh gave up the ghost, he came around briefly. Matron Aisha tried and got him to recall the events that led to the gun shot, fired at him.

'Who shot you, Doctor?' Aisha asked, taking on the approach as the Vice President had directed her

'The policewoman.' Idoh's voice was feeble.

'Is it the policewoman or the First Lady?'

'It is the policewoman.'

'Why?' Aisha pretended to be showing concern.

'I shot Maggy.' His voice was heavy. The breath had irregular rhythm.

'Why did you shoot the First Lady?'

'She had HIV.'

'I don't get you, Doctor.'

'Maggy was HIV positive, we didn't want her husband to know . . . .' Idoh forced out the words, and stopped as he felt a tremor in his body and a lump in his mouth.

'Why won't you want the president to know?' Idoh's confirmation of the AIDS rumour in the presidency since the death of Maggy did not surprise Aisha. She knew it was what Ahmed wanted. She waited for Idoh, gave him time to gather more strength to speak. If they both didn't want the President to know about her ailment, then there must be something else. If there was consensus there couldn't be a conflict, simultaneously.

'If both of you agreed, there was no argument. There was no reason for you to shoot her.' Asiha probed further.

Idoh heard her but he could not talk again, the mouth was filled with blood, the strength was gone. He merely shook his head in disagreement with Aisha. In an attempt to open his mouth, blood, thick and crimson-like, came out and his eyes were wide open, unblinking. One heavy last gasp to hold on to live, and he stopped breathing. Forever.

It was at this point that Aisha called Ahmed to inform him of the critical condition of Idoh and down loaded for him the scanty information she got from the doctor before his last breath.

xxxxx

Mark and Ahmed got to the National Hospital simultaneously. Their two personal assistants were with them.

'If need be, we must fly him out for treatment.' Mark told Ahmed. 'He must not die.'

'There is nothing we can do, Sir. The hospital said the condition is hopeless.' Ahmed was already aware of the situation.

'I wish he lived. He's such a devoted friend until the recent events.' Mark was almost talking to himself.

Vice President Mando could not believe he had Mark properly. How could he have kind words for the man who supposedly pulled the trigger that killed his wife? 'Maybe death this way is better than the type of death for murderers.'

'It would have been better if we had him talked about what went wrong.' Mark pretended not to be in clear picture of all that happened. He thought there was the need to handle the issue carefully. He knew it could jeopardise his chance or that of the party at the polls. Ahmed, here, he thought, would quickly seize the advantage any slip or scandal would offer.

'It must be serious to have taken this proportion and dimension, Mr. President.' Ahmed studied the countenance of his boss. He could not read anything in it.

'The public is waiting for him to tell the world why he killed my wife.'

'Now, that he's gone?' Ahmed put in simply.

'I don't know exactly what to tell the public.'

'Gossip columns in the dailies are saying something about an affair between them.' Ahmed paused. When Mark did not respond, he continued. 'We can toe that line in government's release to the press.'

'I wouldn't like to discredit my wife, even in death.' Mark said slowly, but he was very hurt, inside. 'Maggy had been a most faithful wife since we got married. I am hundred per cent sure about her fidelity.'

The VP considered this. The President was sure of Maggy. Where did she catch the bug? From Mark of course. The President must be HIV positive. His Excellency's must have developed into AIDS. 'I am sorry to say that, Sir. I was only thinking of solving the mystery or bury it altogether. The second option seemed to be the most feasible, in the light of present circumstances.'

President Okuta saw the political undertone of his deputy from the analysis. 'This cannot be buried, Ahmed. It is a measurable quantity. We cannot give half-truth, a quarter truths, but the whole-truth, the total truth. That's what must be gunned for in this case so that all rumours would be laid to rest.'

Ahmed nodded in agreement. He didn't know what else to say. They entered the reception of the National Hospital. Labake Pedro and Susan Okoh, their personal assistants followed them. Inside the special male ward, the nurses were busy packing up the remains of Doctor Bibilari.

xxxxx

Three weeks had gone by since the death of Idoh, three weeks of unchecked press freedom to publish and recycle stories on the death of Maggy and Idoh. The thoroughly investigative piece that appeared in *The Spectator* newspaper had all the trappings and qualities of good journalism but stood on a faulty thesis: age-long illicit affair between Maggy and Idoh.

The reporters got their facts right on the campus relationship between Idoh and Maggy before Mark, the Saint, came on board. Idoh had been slow to tell Maggy his intention. Maggy was stunning in her beauty, brilliant in her academics, bright in her outings and bold in her utterances. She was a darling of every man in her final year in college. Before Idoh could wake up from being a handsome gentleman, the cowboy-like, self-assertive Mark had come in like Zorro and swept Maggy off her feet. Willingly. Despite this competitive victory and loss in the game of love, Mark and Idoh remained the best of friends on the campus and their good relationship continued after they both left the popular University of Zowambia.

The newspaper insinuated that Idoh took a wife and settled down quickly to family life in order to avoid the pang of jealousy and envy building up in him. As expected, Idoh's disposition lured him into staying on in the University, drawn into the atmosphere of scholarship and rectitude while Mark catapulted himself into the turbulent and unsure terrain of politics after graduating from law school. The investigative piece asserted that it was the undying love and the illicit meetings of Idoh and Maggie rather than the friendship loyalty that got Idoh the physician's job at the Presidency. The paper quoted Matron Aisha Rilwan that HIV status of the First Lady led to the argument between them and the gun shots by him. It was therefore not unlikely that the virus was donated to the late First Lady her by Idoh or Mr. President. It could only be from any of the two sources, the investigative report concluded. Despite this headline of imaginary love affair with Idoh, all Zowambians regarded Maggy as a woman of high moral standard.

The speculation that President Okuta was HIV positive was going round in the country to the extent that some foreign allies of Zowambia asked the President to submit himself for a test. The HIV status of his late wife, which he had tactically admitted and the fact that she was carrying a three-months old pregnancy, made all explanation, by the Presidency, that Mark was okay, untenable. The press conference granted by Health Minister could not douse the call for the President to go for a test or admit his status and commence treatment. There was political undertone in every attack on the presidency over his health.

Mark listened attentively to the press interview granted by his Health Minister. After submitting to the press that the likelihood of the late First Lady's HIV status did not automatically translate to the husband and children being HIV positive, the minister wanted them to know that it was just another ailment. It thus had nothing to do with leadership or position.

'What comes to your mind when you are confronted by HIV/AIDS victims?' the first correspondent asked.

Health Minister Bitrus Bewang considered the question before answering. 'It all depends on the circumstance. Sexual irresponsibility, bad-luck or ill-luck, pity, stay-clear-of-him—are some of the things that come to mind.'

'Would you recommend an AIDS victim to be saddled with the pressure that the job of a busy administrator demands?' A second reporter asked.

'Why not, if he is physically fit and such victim has a strong body constitution that won't give way to depression because of his condition?'

The next question came from *The Mirror*. It was more direct. 'Is it good for Zowambia to be ruled by a man who is likely to be HIV positive?'

Bitrus smiled. The demand that Mark should not run for a second term because of the circumstances on ground started from the tabloid. Bitrus knew the newspaper was run by politicians opposed to Mark. 'There is no big deal in being HIV-positive. A person infected with the human immune-deficiency virus could stay healthy throughout his life without becoming an AIDS victim. Many Zowambians are HIV positive without knowing it.' He paused.

'You have not answered the question.' Another correspondent spoke.

Bitrus decided to throw up a challenge. 'The late First Lady was said to be HIV positive. She could have become infected from any of the media of infection—sex, sharp objects, injections or other treatments. She was a healthy person. Likewise if the President by virtue of association was unlucky to have contacted the bug, there's no sign of disability in him not to function as President.'

'What of the stigma?'

'That's the problem of the unenlightened individuals.' Bitrus replied the person that interrupted from the stands.

'The individuals are in the majority.'

'Then let them decide who to rule them at the polls: a HIV-positive suspect individual who is a competent manager of resources or political jobbers who would squander the resources?'

'What are you suggesting, Sir?' *The Times* reporter asked.

'I am not a politician, ladies and gentlemen of the press.' Bitrus looked across the crowded press room and saw Labake Pedro frowning. Whatever it was he must have said that was not okay could not be retrieved. He decided to continue. 'But the fourth estate of the realm could help set the standards for politicians who aspire to elected post. Review their qualifications, compare them and give the true picture to the public to decide.'

'Last question, please.' The press aide attached to the minister said.

It was *The Mirror* man that jumped to his feet again. 'Is the President HIV-positive?'

'Based on the last test conducted on him, two years ago, he was HIV-negative.' Bitrus paused. 'A new test has to be conducted to answer your question. To put it simply I am not sure of his HIV-status now. Thank you.'

The crowd dispersed after this. Labake walked to the minister in the parking lot. 'You should have told them that President Okuta is HIV-negative.'

'I am a doctor, madam. It is unethical to confirm a health situation one doesn't know much about. Besides, I didn't see the papers from a competent doctor to confirm your claim.' Bitrus insisted.

'Where is your loyalty, Minister?'

'I am completely loyal to the President.' Bitrus lowered his voice. 'It will take a fresh test to convince the people. The cover-up done on the status of the late First Lady would make an average Zowambian to conclude that the latest one, secretly conducted, was full of intentional deception,' he paused. 'That's why I did not mention it.'

Labake considered his statements. 'What do you suggest?'

'If you are sure of the President's latest status, you can go ahead and arrange another test, provided he would agree. The presidency could use the advantage of incumbency to influence the electoral commission to make it mandatory for other presidential candidates to go for the same screening of their blood samples.

'That's a good idea,' Labake was sure Mark would still test negative.

'The alternative was that the President could decide not to do the test and challenge other candidates to tell the electorate their status, with evidence from competent medics.'

Labake smiled. 'That's a bright idea, Mr. Bewang. Nobody wants to try the test. The fear of the unknown is feasible in everybody. I remember that at the flag-off of the AIDS campaign two years ago, only ten volunteers stepped forward after Mark had submitted himself for the test.' She smiled again. 'The presidential candidates will turn away from HIV and focus on other fundamental issues that could win them nomination and consequently, election.' She made to go. 'We'll see later in the day at the Council of State meeting.'

'One important thing the President must know, madam.' Bitrus stopped. Labake looked at him expectantly but he took his time, considering how to put his words across, before speaking. 'Since the HIV status of late Maggy was confirmed and she was three months pregnant, it means the president had fun with her less than four months ago. The infection on President Mark might still be in the incubation period. It is only after six months of the last contact between them that a meaningful test could be conducted.'

'Then, you want the test delayed.' Labake put in thoughtfully.

'If His Excellency wants to be completely sure he is free or not, he only could decide on the test-date.' Bitrus further posted.

'I think you are right.' Labake was calculating the possible date for the test, and it must be six months after the last sexual contact between the couple. But she was sure the President's test would be negative again. If on the contrary, it was positive, then she would have become one of the victims of Idoh. She grimaced but remained unperturbed. 'I will explain your line of thought to the President.

'That'll be fine, madam.' Bitrus took his file used for the press briefing and moved towards the exit door. 'I'll check on the staff of the Fortress Clinic before I go.'

Labake was half listening. Her mind had gone to other matters. Lisa Pedro had been picked up by the Central Intelligence Department of the police to re-explain her role on the day Maggy was killed. The sustained interest of the CID was a surprise to her, more so, as Lisa was one of them. She thought it must be true that Vice President Ahmed was behind the unrelenting effort of the investigating team to unravel the cloudy areas of the tragedies.

Felix Aki, *The Mirror* reporter, was not happy that the press conference did not address any new development on the death of Maggy. He wanted something new for the next day's edition. He had thought earlier that if expert interrogators stepped in and worked on Lisa, she could still have more useful information on the issue. The Vice President had bought the idea from a hard working reporter who had his eyes on the prestigious and plum job of press officer in the presidency. Initially, Ahmed didn't want his campaign organisation to rough-handle Lisa. She had been his wife's police aide until Alimot dropped her. Hajiya Alimot Mando had suspected that the policewoman was having an affair with the Vice President. She was right.

Two men and two women who had served in the Army Intelligence unit were given the assignment. They were members of Ahmed's campaign organisation. They posed like police officers from the CID and took Lisa to a private building while the press briefing of the Health Minister was on. Felix knew the hideout and headed for the place after Bitrus' briefing. He was admitted into another room where the interrogation was to be monitored on the screen. Barely seconds after Felix settled down, the interrogation started. He could see that Lisa looked unruffled. There was no fear in her. She must have known that her interrogators would not use any of the biafran tactics to extract the truth from her. Felix believed that her composure had to do with her close relationship with the Vice President. He was brought back from his review of the love affair between Lisa and Ahmed when the face of Lisa came up on the screen.

Two of the interrogators—a male and a female—were on her immediately she sat down. 'Why were you dropped by the Second Lady?' The male interrogator started the interrogation. Alimot Mando was referred to as the second lady by the general public.

Lisa smiled. 'You should ask the Inspector General. He posted me there and later redeployed me.'

'Alimot said that you were not concentrating on your job.' The female interrogator put in.

'That was her opinion. I read in the gossip column of *The Mirror* that Her Ladyship saw my concentrated look on her husband during a state function and later accused me of being distracted to perform my duty effectively.'

'Don't you think that you eventually lost concentration and allowed Lady Maggie Okuta to be killed?'

'I wasn't in the room.' Lisa paused. 'The First Lady asked me out of the room.'

'Is that supposed to be so?'

'I raised an eyebrow in protest but she told me she needed some privacy with the family doctor.'

'How did you get deployed to the late First Lady?'

'I was on leave, my annual leave. My sister-in-law called me to report to her office for a special assignment.'

'Continue.'

'I reported for duty as directed.'

'On the day the president's wife was murdered?'

'Yes.'

'You replaced her police aide?'

'Yes.'

'Did you know why?'

'I was told it was a temporary assignment to stand in for the injured aide of the First Lady.'

'Who told you that?'

'Mrs. Labake Pedro.'

'She chose you for the job because she knew the First Lady will be killed and she wanted you to cover their plot.'

'Their plot?' Lisa was lost. 'Whose plot?' she asked, bewildered.

The female interrogator answered. 'President Mark and your sister-in-law.'

'I don't think they hatched any plot.' She paused. 'For whatever reason, the late doctor shot at the First Lady twice before I could stop him.'

'How did you know he was going to shoot her?'

'The personal assistant to the president and the Chief Security Officer made that possible.'

'The room was bugged. Is that what you are saying?'

'I was equipped.'

'Somebody knew something was going to happen and that somebody didn't prevent it.' The male interrogator looked intensely at Lisa. 'As a law officer, don't you think the President and Labake should be questioned over the shootings and the consequences?'

'I am sure they had revealed what prompted their decision in separate interviews.'

'You think the public is satisfied with their explanation?

'In a way, I think so.' Lisa was looking thoughtful. 'It was when the blood issue and politics were mixed that doubts of their sincerity began to germinate in a few minds, especially through the insistence of *The Mirror* reporter.'

Felix smiled, as he watched from the other room.

'Since you overheard the last conversation between the two, what was the main contention between them?'

Lisa adjusted herself on the seat, almost sitting on the edge. 'I have answered this question several times.' She looked from one interrogator to the other, and started to pick her words, slowly and clearly. 'There was no contention. Doctor Idoh must have revealed to the First Lady her HIV status and how she got infected. I didn't know the detail as my gadget was malfunctioning. But I am sure she was annoyed and felt humiliated. She was at the point of calling her husband when Idoh shot her. The pitch of the argument at that point made my receiver came to live and I entered the room, though a bit too late.'

'Who was responsible for her infection?'

Lisa was silent.

'Who was responsible? Who gave her the bug?' the male interrogator asked in a harsh, commanding tone?

'The President will tell you who gave the bug to our dear Maggy when he is ready.'

'You mean to say when he is completely sure that the blood sample of Maggy does not exist anywhere again.'

'The President has not denied Maggy's status.' Lisa defended Mark.

'He has not openly acknowledged it either,' the female interrogator put in.

'I think he was waiting for the right time to do it. There may be more to his silence than his own HIV status.' Lisa offered her informed opinion.

'There you are, defending the HIV President again?'

'You are not sure of what you are saying.'

'It is you and your sister-in-law only that are still protecting the President. HIV is like a sore on the backside that could not be hidden from public gaze.' A third interrogator who had joined them stated.

'Can I go, please?' Lisa asked them.

'One last question, Lisa,' the fourth interrogator who came in to the room put in. 'Where is the recorded conversation between Idoh and Maggy?' The elderly man held her hands in his, tightening the grip progressively.

Lisa thought of how to put her words neatly. She was going to stay between lie and truth. It was the first time she was asked the question on the whereabouts of the tape. But the truth was that she did not know what happened to the tape. 'I set it concealed on the table as was directed. It became difficult to know who picked it as everybody concentrated on the dying first lady and Doctor Bibilari. Whoever picked it was neither the President nor his personal assistant.' She stopped, and observed the interrogators were satisfied with the response. The shifting movements in their eyes told her so.

'Why are you so sure the President or his P.A. didn't pick it?'

Lisa thought the question offered her an opportunity to strengthen her position on the issue. 'Yes, Mrs. Pedro asked for the tape, the day after Maggy's death. I didn't have the tape, and I told her so. And that was the truth.'

Lisa stood up and followed her interrogators to the door. One of them told her they might contact her again. She advised them to prosecute her in the court of law if they have any incriminating evidence against her on the events of that fateful day. As she was clear of the downtown questioning apartment, she made up her mind to ask the Vice President to help influence her posting outside Seaview City. She would prefer Golas or Portogas or the peaceful city of Santa-bad. She became more interested, than she had ever been, to reconcile with her estranged lover. The Vice President would not help if he sensed she wanted to go back to Gabriel. Men are jealous and selfish. Politicians inherit the vices in double dose. The vices turn to chronic diseases in some of them. Ahmed Mando is one. She mused on.

xxxxx

Labake reported to the President on the press briefing by the Health Minster. After listening to her, Mark concluded that the briefing wasn't necessary. The British press and a section of Zowambia press, aided by public opinion and circumstantial evidences available to them, had concluded that the death of Maggy was a conspiracy between Idoh, Labake and himself.

Mark was silent for a while before he responded. 'The three of us knew about the blood sample that belonged to Maggy, the test that was carried out and the result.' Mark stopped. He wanted to continue and explain his meeting with the British ambassador to Zowambia, but the feeling of some pains on his forehead prevented him.

Labake observed his countenance. 'You look terrible, Mr. President.' She paused as he managed to smile. 'You need some rest. You could designate the VP or the various ministers to handle your appointments for the rest of the day.'

'It is your duty.' Mark smiled again. He believed that smile eases tension. He needed it more than any analgesic to get him back to his table. A lot had gone wrong since he asked the vice president to send Maggy's blood sample to London. He had slipped in his duties. Errors had been committed. That's how Tony Whitesand, the envoy, put it. 'Let the vice president handle every assignment for the rest of the day.' Mark added after his thoughtful silence.

Labake nodded in agreement. 'At least, it will take him away from partisanship for a few hours.'

Mark did not comment further. He stood up and left the office. Labake called the Fortress clinic to alert them that the president needed medical attention.

xxxxx

Shortly after the president left, the arrival of a delegate of traditional rulers from Gadas Local Government was announced. Labake directed the protocol officer to send them to the Vice President's office.

She called the vice president to intimate him with the latest development. 'The President said you should handle his assignments for the day.'

'Is he travelling?' Ahmed was surprised. He usually got selective assignments nowadays. Not all presidential duties.

'He is around.' Labake considered her next words. 'He is a bit indisposed.'

'His indisposition is becoming frequent.' Ahmed told her.

'Is that supposed to be a compliment or a complaint?' Labake's voice sounded on the side of bitterness than annoyance. She knew Ahmed's relationship with her sister-in-law, Lisa. She had wondered why he had to be the one trying to implicate her on the death of Idoh and Maggy. Labake knew that the man on the other end of the line could do anything to satisfy or realise his political ambition. Lisa could go to jail if that would help his presidential aspiration in the Zowambia National Party.

Ahmed was surprised at her question. 'Mrs. Pedro, you are talking to the Vice President.'

Sir,' she paused. 'Your question was a bit sarcastic on your boss.'

The Vice President pondered her statement. He decided to leave it lat that for a while. 'I am not complaining about the President's illness, I am only expressing my concern.'

'Oh, I see.'

Ahmed cut in. 'You don't understand my worries, Labake.' He paused and spoke again with emphasis on every word. 'As a result of recent happenings, the president should watch his health.'

'What do you suggest? He should go for a check-up overseas?'

'If it is headache again,' Ahmed paused, and continued, 'I will strongly suggest that the President send his blood sample for a comprehensive test.'

'To check whether it is HIV or typhoid or . . . '

'It is your words, Labake, not mine.' Ahmed suppressed his smile and partial triumph. He had wanted to tell the President to submit himself for a test to enable the National Party delegates know that their President was still eligible for re-election at party and country levels.

'I will forward your advice to the President.' She smiled, a little uncomfortably. 'Meanwhile, I will join you to welcome the royal fathers from Gadas.'

As Labake dropped the phone handle on its cradle, she reviewed her discussion with Vice President Ahmed Mando. She knew that the bloodgate scandal and HIV issue would play prominent roles in the electioneering campaign for the party ticket. President Okuta had promised to let her know if he would vie for re-election after the meeting with the British and US envoys. Mark had met with them but he had not given her his decision after the two important meetings. Instead, he came out with a headache, a bad one that made him look pale and a few years older than his age. She stood up and resolved to take the advice of the Health Minister in the issue at hand. If HIV status would determine who hoisted the National Party's flag in the presidential election, let the four candidates submit for the test. She smiled and walked out spiritedly, across the lawn, to the vice president's office.

xxxxx

Mark was looking fit again after forty eight hours rest. Labake had visited him in the presidential villa of the Fortress twice daily. The rest had restored his vitality. Labake was in his room at 10 p.m on her way to her own official quarters. Since the death of Maggy, the care of the President had fallen on domestics servants. By mutual unspoken consent, the two had not renewed their relationship. Labake felt guilty that Maggy died on the particular day she shared Mark with her. The latter was a bit lost without Maggy for she had been a pillar stabilising the husband's political career. He had decided to honour her by abstaining from any relationship for a while.

Now in pajamas, and fully rested, Labake's entrance into his room aroused some desire in him. She looked beautiful and stress-free. She must have repaired her make-up as she closed for the day. Most women normally do so to hit the road in order not to look tired and rough. Labake looked younger in her tight-fitting oganza dress that showed all her curves. The president concentrated his looks at the vital areas peeping out in her chest and desire flooded his entire being. Where the President lay on the bed, Labake saw the movement under his clothes. 'You are really out of your illness, Mark.' she smiled looking at the bulging area between his legs.

'That one is not in the body.' He tried to reprimand the offending intruder with his left hand, it is in the mind.' He paused. 'I think the man is protesting for a little action.'

Labake almost laughed. 'Tell the man that the mourning is not over yet. He should stay sober for three months as a sign of loyalty to the demised owner.' She stopped and they both laughed.

Mark took his drugs before Labake left for her apartment, a kilometre distant away in the Fortress. He had expressed his gratitude and appreciation to her for insisting that he should take complete rest. He had become healthier and the affairs of the presidency had not suffered. He closed his eyes and tried to concentrate on recalling the dialogue between him and the British envoy, Tony Whitesand.

Tony had not believed that Idoh killed Ivy Douglas. The autopsy conducted on her remains concluded it was cardiac arrest. No mention was made of administration of poison But Tony made him realised that the international community was disturbed about the events that led to the death of the First Lady, not the isolated incidents of Ivy's death.

'When did you know about your wife's HIV-status, Mr. President?' Envoy Tony Whitesand had asked.

'That was after her accident in Longbridge.' Mark remembered that he didn't want to be specific.

'Did she tell you herself?'

'No.'

'Who told you, Sir?'

'Doctor Ivy Douglas of Embassy Hospital.'

In five minutes, he narrated in details all that happened between the time the blood sample was requested from Zowambia and the return of Maggy to Seaview city, near Longbridge.

'It was after my secretly-conducted blood test that I asked Idoh to let the First Lady know about her HIV status. I thought it would be easier for her to face our doctor. I planted the tape on her in order to know the details.' Mark concluded his narration, opened his top drawer and brought out the tape and recorder. He inserted the tape and put it on play mode. One minute, two minutes gone, and nothing came out. Fast forwarded, still nothing. The reverse side had nothing on it, too. Mark examined the tape critically. Yes it was the tape. What must have happened? He was sweating and Tony Whitesand had seen his mounting anxiety.

'There is nothing in that tape, Mr. President.'

'There was recorded voice of late Idoh, Maggy, Labake, Lisa and mine on it. I listened to it a day before Maggy's burial.'

'Somebody must have replaced it with another, then.' Tony suggested.

Mark had re-examined it. 'It is the same one.'

'Then it had been wiped clean.'

'Who could that be?' Mark was thoughtful.

'It could be you, Labake or Lisa if the game is to continue to protect your own HIV status and your involvement in the killings, as alleged by your opponents, the non-partisan public and the press. On the other hand, the opposition's need for it could be to expose or blackmail you into not contesting for a second term.'

'Who cleaned up the recorded voice?' Mark wondered aloud.

'That's the big question, Your Excellency.' Tony responded. 'Knowing who did it would not change the situation because the evidence is gone.' You have only one option.' He stopped.

'What's the option?'

'Go for the HIV test if you are sure it will be negative. If otherwise, all the crimes, allegedly committed by Idoh would be placed on your doorstep. Your personal assistant will be seen as an accomplice.'

Mark looked thoughtful. 'I think I will do that.'

Tony stood up to go as Mark stopped pacing the room. He peeped through the window curtain and saw a bird trying to walk on the artificial lake. Suddenly, water from the fountain splashed on its body. In its attempt to take off it slid further into the lake and started to drift with the induced water current. How will it get itself out of the wet situation? Mark was full of pity for the bird that could not use its wet wings and entangled legs. He tried to force a smile as he reflected on his own predicament.

'Please, find out what happened to the tape, Mr. President.' Tony said, and brought back Mark's attention.

'I'll do so. It is top priority.' Mark assured him as he took his exit.

He became tired and sad. He had sunk into his chair and covered his eyes with both hands, ready to weep out his sorrow if the tears would come. He was emotionally sad.

xxxxx

The headlines of Zowambia dailies were almost the same on the day Mark resumed work: the presidency and its HIV problem. The newspapers insinuated, and in some cases, affirmed that President Mark was hiding in order to avoid presenting the evidence that would exonerate or implicate him and his aides on the murder of the First Lady and the family physician.

Labake got hold of *The Mirror* and quickly crossed over to the President's office. There was a need to talk on the issue raised by the news in the papers before Mark got too busy.

'What do we do?' Mark asked.

'Let's release the content of the tape.' Labake suggested. 'It will put a stop to these speculations and accusations. Besides, it may put an end to the clamour for you to retake the test.'

The president was silent.

Labake wondered why there was no response to her suggestion 'What do you think, Mr. President?'

Mark did not know what to say. He knew that Labake did not tamper with the tape. He had tried all possibilities from his sick-bed but he could not get any clue to whoever erased the tape. It didn't just go bad, he was convinced. He smiled to ease his sadness and responded, 'I don't have the tape, Labake.'

'You don't have the tape?' Labake almost shouted.

'Yes.' Mark met the probing eyes of his assistant. 'Somebody had tampered with the tape.' He stopped. Labake was dumfounded. She quickly lowered herself into the nearest seat, bowed her head and supported it with both hands. 'I discovered its loss of audio when I wanted to play it to the hearing of the British envoy.' Mark tried to break the silence that enveloped the room.

'I could now understand why you turned white after Envoy Whitesand departed your office.' She raised her head and stood up.

Mark nodded his head. 'I am trying to find out who did it.'

'We don't have all the time, Mr. President. Your party convention is next week-end. Ten days from now.'

'I am aware of that.'

'What good will knowing the perpetrator does to your name and candidacy?' Labake considered the implications of the loss of Idoh's confessional statement.

'At least the intruder would tell us and the world what he learnt form the tape. It would support my claim, yours and Lisa's.'

Labake frowned 'The public will still hold on to their view that our claim of your negative status is a cover up.'

'I have made up my mind to take the test again, two days before the convention. That's what I told the envoy.'

'If that be the case, we could use the power of incumbency to force other candidates to take the HIV test.' Labake submitted.

'And you think they will do so?'

'They flew the kite; they must watch the movements in the sky, too.' She was sure the other aspirants in the National Party would not buy the idea of going for HIV test. None of them had voluntarily submitted to do so in the past nationwide campaign against HIV/AIDS. Since HIV had become a factor in the political equation, everybody in the supremacy game in the political classroom must be involved in solving the equation. The idea of extending such idea to the election proper after the primaries fascinated her. To her, it didn't mater anymore, who the virus consumed politically.

Mark bought the idea. 'I foresee that this election will help to bring on board a government that will be conscious of HIV/AIDS and, thus, work towards curtailing and preventing the scourge.'

Labake smiled and stood up. She would involve the Health Minister whose idea it was, originally. She would also investigate who could have tampered with the tapes. Idoh had tampered with the blood samples by eliminating those who knew about it besides herself and the president, she concluded within herself.

She was called at the international reception room of the Fortress to inform her of the arrival of the Canadian envoy. The stories on the blood sample were bringing various groups to Seaview Fortress.

The Information Minister, Garba Malik, left Labake's office fully briefed on how to handle the campaign strategy of President Okuta for the party primaries. As the designated head of Mark Okuta Campaign Team, MOCT, Garba called on *The Mirror* newspaper and told the editor the need to make it mandatory on whoever wanted to be president to be comprehensively checked, health-wise. The editor bought the idea and it appeared in the editorial opinion of the newspaper the following day. Simultaneously Garba and Bitrus presented a joint bill to the National Assembly on the minimum health standard of the president and the governors. They deliberately left out the assembly members in order to facilitate the passing of the bill into law.

The Democrats were enthusiastic about the bill. The upper and lower houses would have gone on recess from that day but for the urgency of the bill. The Democrats saw it as an opportunity to eliminate Mark from contesting the coming election as an incumbent. The initial protest by the majority National party members frizzled out the next day. The Vice President had lobbied them to pass the bill into law. Ahmed had thought it would favour him in the process if Mark, out of fear, decided not to take the test.

The bill was passed by the upper and lower houses of assembly, barely four days to the primaries of the National Party. President Mark Okuta signed it into law and declared that he was ready for the test. He expressed his hope that the other candidates would submit themselves for the test too. His decision rattled the Vice President who thought Mark would back out.

The Zowambia Electoral Commission put together a medical team comprising doctors and para-medics from both parties and some non-partisan professionals to jointly conduct the test on the presidential aspirants who were expected to submit themselves for the test to comply with the law promulgated. Such exercise was initially declared voluntarily compulsory by the Electoral Commission of Zowambia.

xxxxx

The latest development on getting tested did not go well with the National Party presidential candidates. One of them, Doctor Donatus Zango, during his campaign rally, attempted to pull out of the race rather than submit himself for a test that would be manipulated from the incumbent or the vice president, he argued.

The implication of his withdrawal on his political career made him soft-pedal and allowed reason to prevail.

'As a medical doctor you ought to encourage to be interested in knowing their status.' *The Mirror* had challenged him.

'I am healthy as you can see.' He made a body movement to demonstrate his strength and the healthy looking muscles of his arms. 'It is those who are likely to be infected, going by their family history that should be tested.'

Are you saying the President alone should go for the test?' *The Spectator* correspondent asked him. 'It means you want to go to the elections without taking the test.' *The Mirror* man stated.

'All the Democratic Party aspirants are going to their convention tomorrow without subjecting themselves to the test.' Donatus tried to support his stand on the issue.

'You know it is a big risk being taken by that party. Whoever emerges tomorrow will still have to go for the test to qualify for the election proper.' *The Weekly Sweeper* correspondent explained to candidate Donatus.

Donatus smiled. 'We shall get ready to cross the bridge upon arrival at the river bank.'

His wider grin was shot-lived as party supporters in his campaign rally shouted their opposition to the rooftop.

The following day, he accepted to submit himself for the examination if the Zowambia Electoral Commission would ensure that credible doctors and non-partisan lab-technicians would conduct the test.

The other candidate, Idris Karfi, accepted to take part, provided that the blood samples would be taken at the same time, properly labeled by separate team and passed over to another team for the test proper.

Vice President Mando kept silent on the issue. ZNP agreed that the tests would take place the following Monday, after the week-end primaries of the Democratic Party, a day before their own primaries.

xxxxx

The Democratic Party held its Convention inside the main bowl of the National Stadium in Longbridge. As expected, Yusuf Naibawa won the election to fly the flag as their presidential candidate. He was neither the most experienced nor the most qualified of the contestants, but the one that came from the zone to which the party decided the next president should come from. His main rival Austin Njoku, whose civil service outstanding performance and whose stewardship in the various positions he held was not tainted with corruption and nepotism, was sacrificed on the altar of zonal consideration.

In his acceptance speech, Yusuf enjoined all the aspirants who contested with him to let them work together as a team and dislodge the National Party of President Okuta from the Seaview Fortress.

To end his acceptance speech as the presidential candidate, he charged up the atmosphere with statements and questions that marked his consequent rhetoric at the soap-box.

'Four years ago, Mark promised us light, uninterrupted electricity generation, but all we've got since, is darkness.' Yusuf's voice reverberated in the whole arena.

'Yes.' The crowded arena agreed.

'Four years ago, Mark promised to create employment for at least forty per cent of unemployed college graduates, did he fulfil this promise?

'No.' the crowd responded.

'They promised us adequate, clean water supply but the taps are most of the time dry, and whenever it flows, the water is polluted.'

'Yes.'

'Mark promised to end ethnic conflict across Zowambia. Did he deliver on his promise?'

'No, no, no.'

'What of the filthy environment? Is there any improvement now?'

'There is none yet.' Many answered.

'Have they turned the mere consulting clinics that abound in the nation to functional standard hospitals?'

'No.' the delegates shouted.

'They still fly accident victims abroad.' Yusuf Naibawa paused. There was silence as he wiped the sweat on his face with a party handkerchief. 'Recently, Mark's administration had to fly our late First Lady to Europe for treatment at Embassy Hospital in London. We have a National Hospital at Longbrige, and the General Hospitals at Seaview, Golas, Gadas, Oweda, Santa-calab, Charanchi and others. None of these hospitals have facilities for emergency and intensive care.'

There were loud murmurs here and there. He allowed it to ebb before speaking again.

'I wonder where the millions of dollars they budgeted and spent on health care ended in.' Yusuf resumed his speech.

'It ended in their pockets and in their foreign bank accounts.' One party faithful close enough to the microphone shouted and others applauded the comment.

Candidate Naibawa continued. 'As a punishment for their wantonness and corruption, they are now fighting a battle they can not win. They are fighting AIDS in the presidency. They are all infected. The Seaview Fortress occupants are wallowing in health crises but trying to tell Zowambians and the world that all-is-well. Zowambians will no longer entrust the leadership of this country to sick and sickly.'

'Yes.' The delegates chorused.

'Then, go back to your wards, with the reasons the leadership of this nation must change, why the Democratic Party must win the coming election. Let us seize the opportunity of the differences between Mark and his deputy over their handling of the bloodgate, to work hard in the grassroots and take over governance.'

The crowd applauded him again.

'Finally, dear democrats, I want you to believe and have faith in me. I promise to do better than my civil service performance when I get to Seaview Fortress. Supply of utilities will improve, agriculture will take the centre stage from our complete reliance on oil revenue. Food will be cheaper, health delivery will be better, ethnic conflicts will be a thing of the past, quality of education will improve and labour disputes will not be witnessed again. We have the strength, we have the vision, we have the resources and we have a leadership who will be focused on effective and good governance, unlike our rival party leadership that is still busy fumigating its house.

They are busy testing themselves for HIV because they had spent the last four years in a care free style. They are caught in their own corrupt traps. Let us mobilise the masses and go to the polls to roast the remains of whoever they decided to put forward. Thank you.'

The delegates applauded him for a longer time. There was excitement in everyone of them as they thought that the next election would likely produce a Democratic Party president, for the first time since Zowambia jettisoned military rule for true democracy.

xxxxx

The four presidential aspirants of the Zowambia National party came with their supporters and families to the National Hospital venue of the blood test. As expected, a group comprising local and foreign interests made up the diagnostic team.

Supporters of each aspirant were busy outside singing in praise of their aspirant. An atmosphere of hate and distrust was created but the strong presence of the police forestalled any confrontation among the opposing forces. Such was the nature of electioneering process in Zowambia.

The aspirants were briefed on the procedure. The blood samples would be taken simultaneously in separate rooms, and in two sterilized plastic tubes. Candidates would come out together into another room and choose labels discretely for their two samples and put them on the test rack in no particular order. From there, the lab men would commence the test. Only the aspirants would know which result belonged to him when the test procedures were completed.

All of them approved the arrangement.

After emerging from the labeling room and the lab men had taken over, the pressmen cornered each aspirant to find out their expectation.

The Mirror fired the first salvo at Mark Okuta. 'How did you feel coming for the test, Mr. President?'

'The same way you feel, Felix. Full of expectations for bad news.' Mark smiled and patted the reporter on the shoulder. He was remarkable at remembering names.

'The expectation is that President Okuta will test positive.'

'I agree with your expectation, totally.' Mark surprisingly appeared friendly to the reporter who had been very critical of the Presidency's cover-up of the HIV issue.

'The public opinion is that you will test positive, Mr. President.' Felix paused to gauge the reaction of Mark, None was discernible. 'The press predicted you will not turn up for the test.'

Mark almost laughed. 'What do you want me to say again? You've said everything, Felix.'

'Tell me something that the citizens of Zowambia have not heard.

'Then, tell them that it was true that my late wife tested positive but I did not give it to her. Tell them that, initially, I had the proof but unfortunately, I lost it. Whether she infected me with the virus she carelessly—and not promiscuously—acquired, will be known when the latest test result is released. That fifty-fifty chance made the public opinion to be in order. But you journalists goofed in your prediction. Late Maggy and I had been the vanguard in the fight against HIV and AIDS, the virus and its destructive power. If Idoh had not killed Maggy to cover up his professional misconduct and betrayal of friendship, Maggy would have deployed her energy to the prevention of the scourge, using her dual role as a mother and a victim to champion the cause.' Mark paused and examined the spot where the blood was taken from him.

'But it took weeks between the discovery of Her Excellency's HIV status before the rumours started flying around. Don't you think, Sir that the press was given the opportunity to insinuate rightly or wrongly?'

'Up to a stage in the saga, I listened to Idoh's advice, partly as a result of my fears because of its political implication and partly because of the diplomatic fury it would generate. Even the victim didn't know until the moment the trigger was pulled by my best friend.'

'Dr Bibilari's involvement made everybody, including your deputy, believe that the killing was done to protect your interest or your secret, your. HIV status.'

Mark made a gesture that he agreed with Felix's statement. 'You may not believe this, Felix,' he started to say, 'I get the pulse of the people through your highly critical medium. Let's forget about the partisanship for a while. I came for the test because people thought I wouldn't risk such a move to make me lose the power that my opponents alleged that I sacrificed my loving wife to retain. But I did come. Though I do not believe that HIV status should debar anybody from aspiring to any position in the society, I will not contest the primaries of my party if I test positive. I had wanted to have a second term in order to consolidate on the little gains achieved during this tenure. We came from a down below economic basement to the ground level now. Our economic plane is about to take off and as the pilot that brought the plane from the dungeon to the tarmac, I want to be around for a full-throttled take off.' He stopped for breathe.

'But if you test positive and we have that bill already passed into law . . . '

Mark cut in. 'I have said that I will not contest if I am HIV-positive. I will support Vice President Ahmed Mando. He is equally capable. He is ambitious too. I like ambitious men Ambition, enthusiasm are needed on this job. He has both.

'You are already campaigning for him, Mr. President, suppose he tests positive too?'

'Let me tell you this,' Mark noticed that more newsmen were teaming up with Felix, 'the Democratic Party had conducted their presidential primary without going for the HIV test. We all know the implication if Yusuf Naibawa is disqualified on the basis of this.' He paused. 'If I test positive and Ahmed too, or any other aspirant has the bug I will go back to the Assembly and lobby for the removal of that law from our constitution.'

'If it sails through, you'll be able to contest.' *The Spectator* man who had just joined them, observed.

'No, I won't contest if I am HIV positive. Mine will be a moral rather than a political or health question. My status will neither exonerate nor indict me for the deaths associated with Maggy's HIV-status.'

'Your Excellency, supposing Yusuf Naibawa agrees to go for the test?' It was Felix.

'That will be fine. We want more Zowambians to come out and know their status. It is a way to curb the spread. I will still go ahead to lobby for the removal of that law. It is globally unacceptable to stigmatise AIDS victim. HIV and AIDS should be seen like any other ailments. Do you remove a President or disallow a candidate from contesting an election because of his malaria fever, typhoid fever, kidney failure or heart disease? Some of these ailments are more deadly than the virus in question.'

'Why did you sign that bill into law if this is your position on the matter?' The man behind the camera of Zowambia

Independent Television asked, focusing his camera fully on Mark.

'Nobody believed I would come out for the test if it was not passed into law despite my repeated vow that I would do so whenever the arrangement was made. It was my primary reason for sponsoring and supporting the bill. I was not coerced from any quarter apart from journalists. Felix is a typical example.'

There was cordiality devoid of bitterness in the laughter at the mention of *The Mirror's* man.

'Truly the law had helped us to know that the men contesting for my present position in the National Party are men that would truly obey the constitution, men with ambition, who exhibited their bravery to pursue their goal. They all knew the implication of what they did today. No matter the outcome of the tests, any of us is a better candidate than the presidential candidate of Zowambia Democratic Party, who ignored the constitutional provision and went ahead with their primaries.' He paused. 'Good day, gentlemen.'

Mark was gone with Labake and the Information Minister trying to match his strides before the reporters could raise further questions. Felix could not help but admire the President when it came to his discussion of issues with the press. Mark was a reporter's delight, any day, he thought. Felix was beginning to feel that the President was the best candidate for the job.

xxxxx

While President Okuta was busy addressing the joint sitting of the upper and lower houses of Zawambia lawmakers on the need to abrogate his latest bill already passed into law, his first daughter, Perpetua, was taking on Balat Mando on the mystery surrounding the loss of audio of the cassette they had both listened to in the private house of the vice president. Balat was the Vice President's second son, and Perpetua's boyfriend.

Perpetua had grieved with concern over the rumours of her father's involvement in her mum's death. She had laughed it off as a big joke. But, when the news began to make the round in the Vice President's wing of Seaview Fortress, Perpetua had become worried. Balat had asked her to get hold of the tape purportedly recorded at the scene of the crime, and which the president had refused to make public. Her curiosity to know the truth made her to find out more about the tape. Having got a clue of where it was kept, she had bided her time and picked it up when she was alone in her father's office.

Unknown to her, Vice President Mando was interested in the tape too. He had instructed his son to use her relationship with Perpetua to get to the record. It was in Mando's private residence in Seaview City that the pair listened to the recorded voice of her mum and Idoh. She had felt relieved that her father's claim of innocence was true and Idoh's confirmation to Maggy that Mark had just tested negative gladdened her heart. They had both left the tape in his room and had a one-hour swimming training on the premises. Later, she had gone home with the tape and it took her twenty four hours of panic surveillance before she could put it back in the drawer, unnoticed.

Perpetua had felt terribly guilty when Mark told them at breakfast that the loss of audio on the tape was as mysterious and heart-breaking as the death of Maggy. He told the three girls that he would not want to go for a second term, whatever the outcome of the blood test was, unless what disappeared mysteriously reappeared on the tape.

Perpetua was sure her contact with the tape had caused the loss of audio. But she was not sure how it happened. She decided to talk to Balat.

'Have you heard that the audio on the tape vanished?' She asked Balat who met her at the car pack as she was about going to the park.

'You must be joking, darling.' Balat, who suspected what must have happened to the tape, pretended he was unaware of the development.

Perpetua was surprised that Balat didn't know. 'I thought you are current on political issues more than you are exhibiting now.'

He tried not to give himself away. 'I was assuming your dad didn't want to let people know how and who gave the bug to your mum, hence the claim of audio loss on the tape.' Balat lied.

'He was ready to release it to clear his name but for the unexpected that happened to the tape.'

'Who must have wiped out the tape after we played it?' Balat pretended to be in a thoughtful mood.

'That's the million dollar question. I was coming to ask you.'

'You think I did it?'

'You and I had access to the tape. I didn't do it.' Perpetua put it tacitly.

'You think I did it, Perpetua,' Balat's voice carried some anger and disappointment. 'We were both together throughout the period we listened to it. I did not even touch the tape again after we had listened to the content. Remember?'

'Somebody did. Probably, the person did so when we were not there. Remember we left it and went for swimming.' Her voice was sure and convincing. 'Try and help me find out. It could be your dad.'

Balat was shocked at her direct suspicion of his dad.

'Why are you suspecting my dad?'

'He wants to contest against my father in the election. He wants to be the next President.'

'It is a healthy rivalry. A party affair. That's what dad told me.' Balat didn't know what else to say.

'I am sorry, Balat. But I can't help thinking that whoever laid hand on that tape, deleted it in order to give my dad the problem of having to explain all the issues connected with mum's death.

'I agree with you.' Balat was intelligent enough to know that disagreeing with that stated opinion would increase her suspicion of his dad. 'Any of the opponents or competitors within the party could do it. The tape encountered a human virus.'

'That's the best thing you've said since, Balat. Would you help me find out from your dad?'

Balat pondered a while. 'I'll try, but I am sure I wouldn't get anything from him. He wouldn't want me to know he did such a criminal thing. You know politicians. They lead two lives and are highly unpredictable.' He stopped and watched her smiling. 'Why are you smiling? Have I said something wrong?'

'No.' Perpetua who was now convinced that Balat's dad had a hand in the audio loss smiled again. 'Whatever the result of your findings, I am sure you will come out and support me on the content of the tape,' she paused, 'when the time comes, soon.'

'Are you sure that is a reasonable thing to do? Remember that you stole the tape.'

'You asked me to do it.' She looked into his eyes. 'I will not mention the fact that we took it to your private house. If you tell Zowambians what you know was in the tape, your statement will be more credible than mine.' She smiled to his face again.

'My dad may not approve of my doing that.'

'Come on, lover boy, your dad will support you for saying the truth. The Vice President will not support falsehood. Your coming out to speak might enhance his chance.'

'And catapult your dad in a race that he's already in the driving seat.'

Perpetua moved away from the car and he followed her. 'We are not like them, we are not politicians. We are lovers that both sides may not even approve of, with time. Nothing stops us from saying what we know about the blood samples of Maggie, the murderous confessions of a killer doctor and the innocence of Mark.'

'I'll think about that Perpetua.'

'Be fast about it. Whether my dad tests positive or negative, I intend to tell the world what I did with the tape.' Perpetua kissed him lightly on the lips and went back to the car. She was already late for her gymnastic lesson.

xxxxx

President Mark was applauded as he left the National Assembly chamber after his declaration that he was ready to withdraw from contesting the elections as a trade-off for the removal of the obnoxious law that would not stand the test of time or comply with global democratic standards.

He was sure the lawmakers would remove the hurriedly passed law from the constitution. It would be removed before the presidential election. His powerful lobbyist had started working on the assembly men.

He mused at the prospect of an HIV-positive president of Zowambia. Such would give HIV and AIDS the attention it deserved.

As he drove towards the National Hospital, he saw his daughter, Prepetua, in the opposing traffic. Mark wondered why she was late for her gym session. It was unusual of her most favourite daughter.

xxxxx

Balat Mando had a chat with his dad a few hours after his encounter with Perpetua. He had wanted to ask his dad why there was nothing on the tape again. He had not been put into confidence what happened during the hour he had in the swimming pool with Perpetua. Until the reported loss of audio on the tape, he thought the Vice President was merely curious about the content. Wiping it off was a selfish and callous thing to have been done, he concluded within himself. He thought and believed President Okuta had been very magnanimous and fair in his dealings with the Vice President so far.

'Dad,' he called the Vice President's attention as he stood up to go to the bedroom for the night, 'I would like to talk to you on a private matter.'

Ahmed came back to his seat while the others got up and left the room.

'I am listening.' Ahmed relaxed on his seat.

'What did you do to the tape we brought from the president that day, Dad?' Balat stood up from his seat and came to the one next to his dad.

'I listened to the content, that's all.'

'But you dubbed it. I saw the recorder you concealed near the player. It was on as Perpetua and I listened to the tape that day.'

Vice President Mando looked away from his son as he spoke. 'I didn't need it anymore. The content was not useful to my campaign. Hence there was no need to keep the duplicate.'

'But it would help the President to redeem his image.' Balat's tone was accusing. When his father did not respond, he spoke further. 'You wiped off the original copy to frustrate him out of the race, to make his re-election impossible.'

'Who told you I did it?'

'Do I need to be told, dad?' Balat almost shouted. 'The witch shrieked in the night and the child died the following morning.'

'I hope you are not going mad, my dear son.'

'You disappoint me, dad. I want you to be president but I want it done on a level playing ground. I know that the party's political machinery is solidly at your disposal. I still went for the blood sample thing if it would help you to neutralise the incumbency factor. We both knew that the president was innocent. You still went ahead to clean up the evidence.'

'Shut up your mouth and don't mention this again. Didn't you witness all the tactics he employed through the Zowambia Financial Crimes Commission to nail me?'

'That's why you didn't come to his defense in any way, when he was accused of murder.'

'How do I know he wasn't involved? You want me to tell the world I stole his tape through you? Don't be a daft, son.'

'No dad, you could release the tape you dubbed. You still have it, I know.'

'What will you do if I don't release it?'

'I will confirm the President's innocence when Perpetua talks to the press on our handling of the cassette.'

Ahmed was shocked. 'You planned to disgrace me because of the President's girl?'

Balat shook his head. 'No dad, we have a president who is sincere. I want you to listen to his speeches these last few days. You need to learn from him. You need political tutelage from him.' Balat spoke rapidly and ran out of the room.

The Vice President paced up and down the room. He considered what his boy had just said. Maybe, Balat was right after all. He had a sound sleep after he had resolved on what to do.

xxxxx

The Zowambia National Party presidential aspirants met at the National Hospital on the day preceding their primaries in Golas. While the delegates were already pouring to Golas, the combatants sat expectantly, awaiting the results of their HIV tests. The four of them were accompanied by members of their family: Donatus came with his wife, Idris with two of his four wives and his eldest son, Ahmed with his wife and Balat, Mark with Perpetua and her two kid sisters.

The publicity secretary of the Electoral Commission spoke to them as the results were brought in two separate plastic boxes. 'We have two sets of results conducted independently by the two groups. It is heartwarming to discover that they arrived at the same conclusion. Nobody, including those that carried out the tests knew the owners of any particular result, up till now. You selected and coded the blood samples by yourselves. Please, gentlemen, pick your envelopes in both boxes. You are not under any obligation to reveal the result to any body. It is your decision to have the results before your party convention. Thank you.'

President Mark was the first to react. He gave his codes to Perpetua who stood up and picked the result. Vice President Mando followed his example as Balat picked the result up for him. The other two aspirants stood up and picked theirs simultaneously.

Vice President Mando observed that none of them except Mark's daughter opened the envelopes. 'What is the general result like?' He directed his question to the publicity secretary of ZEC.

'Two are HIV positive, two are negative,' he said and stood up, carried the empty boxes and disappeared into an inner room.

President Okuta smiled as he stood up. 'Let us all go and get ready for the journey to Golas, the battle ground for the sole ticket.'

'The battle is going to be between two, the clean two.' Donatus said, trying to open his envelope.

Mark shook his head in disagreement 'The three of you should contest the election. I am sure the HIV test result will not be used to determine who the next president is.'

'What of you?' Ahmed asked.

'I have told you I am not contesting the election, HIV-positive or negative. No more active politcs for me until the public know the truth about Maggy. I wasn't joking or making a political statement earlier.'

'Dad!' Perpetua shouted. 'Both tests are negative.'

'I know that before it was conducted.' Mark was not excited. He turned to others. 'Please, don't reveal your results yet,' he paused, 'for strategic reasons. Perpetua shouldn't have revealed mine. I don't need it.'

'Why are you backing out?'

'I need to convince the world that I did not kill my wife or anybody, in order to cover up my HIV status.'

'You are already vindicated, Sir.' Balat who sat next to his dad, said. 'The Zowambia Independent Television promised to release the recorded voice of Idoh and the late First Lady's tonight. The newscaster said the tape got to their desk miraculously. They wanted to reach the President to verify the content. Lisa Pedro had claimed it was authentic after listening to it at the station.' Balat stopped, and his eyes met those of

Perpetua. The latter was inwardly grateful to him. He looked at his dad and felt proud of him for releasing the tape recording.

Mark and Ahmed exchanged a broad smile as the latter came over to his boss and congratulated him on the double victory. 'You won, Mr. President, you won.'

'Yes and no, Mr. Vice President,' Mark smiled, 'we both won. Let's do it together one more time, the *Mark Ahmed* joint ticket for continuity of the on-going economic reforms.' He had tactically avoided choosing a running mate since the campaign started. The news of the discovery of the tape recording made him decide there and then to run again. He wanted to create the record as the longest, serving democratic President of Zowambia.

'Are you sure you want me to be your running mate after all those volatile hostilities at the soapbox?' Ahmed asked, smiling and looking at the other two candidates who were not surprised at the turn of events.

'I have no choice Mr. VP,' Mark paused. 'Without you beside me, I'll lose in the primaries, either to you or to the expected last minute alliance between Donatus and Idris.'

'Vice President Mando owns the party machinery, Sir.' Donatus pointed out. 'He is the candidate to beat.'

'All the Governors and majority of the legislators and their appointed delegates would definitely file behind him.' Idris supported Donatus view.

'That's why the VP must come in on the joint ticket in order to make it easy for us to defeat Naibawa at the polls.' Mark's voice was appealing, and the three other party men started to laugh simultaneously to the admiration of their families who knew that the blood gate had brought the National Party's presidential aspirants closer and more united in their quest to retain power at the centre.

xxxxx

Before nightfall, Donatus and Ahmed had withdrawn from the primary election. Ahmed had directed all his supporters to vote in favour of the President. From their hotel rooms in Golas, the National Party delegates were unanimous in their opinion that Mark would defeat Idris in the ZNP presidential primary slated for the following day.

'Victory will be ours without any doubt now, Mr. President.' Labake said after briefing Mark on the situation report from Golas.

'Sure banker.' Mark smiled as he looked at his press officer lustfully. 'If the Second Lady will accept the promotion coming to her, it will gladden my heart.'

'So Mr. President knew my nickname in the Fortress.'

'Since our first trip to South Africa.'

'What kind of promotion am I expecting, ministerial again?'

The President grinned. 'The First ladyship,' He observed the surprise look on her and quickly added, 'if you accept the proposal.'

'Wait Mark,' she paused to think. 'Do you want to marry me?'

'Yes.'

'Is it for political reasons?'

'Yes and no. The electorate will frown at a candidate without a complete home. But besides, I love you, Labake. He stood up and held her hands. Are you ready to come on board as the First Lady?'

'No, Mark.'

There was a deep silence between them as Mark considered what to say. It couldn't be that she didn't want to remarry. He was thoughtful. 'Why?' He demanded to know the reason for her refusal.

Labake smiled to ease the tension that her reaction mounted between them before she answered. 'I'll prefer to be Mrs. Mark Okuta.'

They smiled as they instantly locked up in an embrace and followed it up with a long, sensuous demanding kiss that they both knew was the flag off of a two-some night long celebration.

xxxxx

A desperate First Lady ignorantly conspired to fulfill a vital customary obligation to her husband. Scandal was incubated. Two months after the unintended conspiracy, a multiple road accident on the street of Longbridge City involving Her Excellency exposed the hidden. The President's good prospect for re-election was at stake. President Mark Okuta's medical aide became obsessed to cover the viral scandal. *Forward Mark* group set the ball rolling. A series of political intrigues that followed the killing of the First Lady made HIV and AIDS the main election issue in the oil-rich West African country of Zowambia.

The Blood Sample is a political and historical fast paced thriller from the author of *Escape from the South*

www.ingramcontent.com/pod-product-compliance
Ingram Content Group UK Ltd.
Pitfield, Milton Keynes, MK11 3LW, UK
UKHW040015200726
13854UKWH00001B/219

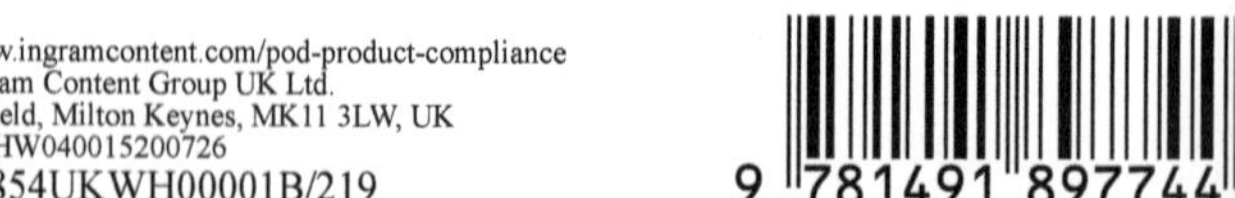

9 781491 897744